The Eleusian Effect

Other Works by Bruce Chester

Great Short Stories

Dadisms

The Steel Age

The Eleusian Effect

Bruce Chester

Published by Bruce Chester
February 2018

First Printing: 2018

ISBN 978-1-387-57066-9

Bruce Chester
30 Pine Street, Suite 310
Gardner, MA 01440

www.bruccchester.com

All characters, events and entities in this book are fictional.

Ordering Information:

Special discounts are available on quantity purchases by corporations, associations, educators, and others. For details, contact the publisher at the above listed address.

U.S. trade bookstores and wholesalers: Please contact Bruce Chester Tel: (978) 514-5500; or email thebenaycompanies@gmail.com

Dedication

To God, for my talent, my family for their love, to my teachers who inspired in me a love of literature.

Table of Contents

Acknowledgements..ix

Chapter 0...x

Chapter 1 The Venus Mission 1

Chapter 2 The Great Conversion 10

Chapter 3 The Adjustment 20

Chapter 4 Revelation 31

Chapter 5 Furlough...34

Chapter 6 First Date 40

Chapter 7 First Date, Second Day.....................................46

Chapter 8 Perfect Nights, Unwanted Attention 52

Chapter 9 The Meeting 61

Chapter 10 More Meetings, Tough Dinners.......................65

Chapter 11 The Mars Mission 72

Chapter 12 An Important Test..81

Chapter 13 Requiem..96

Chapter 14 Mission to Alpha Centauri B.........................108

Chapter 15 Lightspeed..117

Chapter 16 The Arrival 127

Chapter 17 A Galactic Suprise 130

Chapter 18 Marcus 138

Chapter 19 Omnisphere 142

Chapter 20 The Whole Story...148

Chapter 21 The Emissary of Trillian 152

Chapter 22 Exodus 157

Chapter 23 A Grave Decision 162

Chapter 24 The Great Download 168

Epilogue 174

Acknowledgements

I would like to thank everyone who encouraged and inspired me. Thanks to Pete Lincoln, Mrs. McLaughlin my folks and my family.

Chapter 0

I've never liked reading book introductions. If I think it's a good book then I want to get right to the story. So now as an author I decided to do something a little different. Don't worry this is a quick one, more of a disclaimer, really.

This book, The Eleusian Effect is my first. I've used some modern issues and conventions that may look to be an acceptance or promotion of certain things; lifestyles, social issues and such. This is straightforward story where things happen that some may or may not agree with. There are no political statements, no statement for or against any particular group or lifestyle. My views are not expressed in this book as I usually do not try to make any kind of declaration of them in any of my stories. I love a good compelling story and I assume my readers do, too.

So now I am pleased to offer you what I think (and hope) is an entertaining story. I hope you enjoy The Eleusian Effect as much as I did writing it.

Chapter 1

The Venus Mission

June 10, 2169 0530 Hours

It was like nothing anyone had ever seen or experienced. It was 2169. We, the members of GASA (Global Aeronautic and Space Administration) were planning to celebrate the 200th Anniversary of the first manned moon launch. Many of us were inspired by John F. Kennedy's declaration to put a man on the moon, and we would honor that sentiment by putting a man on Venus. We had the technology, but no one could have foreseen, or even imagined what happened when we achieved that dream. We had a crew of 235, 10 bridge crew, and 5 who were senior staff. The senior staff consisted of myself, Chief Medical Officer Darius Barack Obama, the great-great grandson of the 44th President of the United States, First Officer Troy Felloner, Science Officer James Braddock, Telman Harrison, the Chief Engineer and Ship's Captain, Benjamin Tanner. We were all considered text book perfect for this mission; genetically, mentally, and socially. The brass at GASA wanted all single crewmembers, (mostly men) for this mission so there wouldn't be any reason for doubts or hesitations just in case things got difficult.

Our ship, aptly named the USS Kennedy, was state of the art. Once faster-than-light propulsion was discovered, we could explore the galaxy and expand our understanding of the universe. Earth had come a long way and now it was time to see if anyone else was out there. We started with our own solar system. Mars was already 30% colonized and the discoveries of ancient Martian society had changed the attitude of the whole world. So the next step was to see was on the other planet closest to Earth. Little did we know what awaited us on Venus.

The entire mission was a mere month. The goal was to return home by July 20. Almost routine, the journey to Venus would only last a few hours. It was simple: go to Venus, do a standard planet evaluation and come home. For all intents and purposes that's what we did. On June 16, 2169, the Kennedy was launched from the

Orbital Space Platform Reagan. The Saturn 12 Propulsion system was the main engine for the Kennedy and we had 6 operating in tandem. This was more than enough power to get us there and to get us home. The Kennedy was reminiscent of a fictional spaceship on an ancient television program. It had several amenities and a perfected anti-gravity system so it was not only powerful but comfortable. It had 6 land vehicles with short term orbital capability and 25 escape pods. It was a more than adequate ship. This is my personal log so I will be recording all significant events here.

LAUNCH DATE: JUNE 16, 2169
LAUNCH TIME: 0600 GMT

The Kennedy performed a textbook launch from the pad. Orbital Reagan was the newest platform and it performed without a flaw. The Kennedy left space dock 7A and proceeded to FTL-1 once it cleared the atmospheric margin. The margin is a safety measure in order to prevent FTL ships from potentially tearing the atmosphere off the planet. It's highly unlikely, but GASA and the Global Leadership thought it a practical decision. We had spent decades trying to fix the environment after the Plasma Wars almost ruined it. Can't blame them for being cautious.

I was hoping for an uneventful trip. The Kennedy's crew was relatively new, so this mission will give them a little time to get to know each other. Hopefully, it will be a solid crew for future missions. GASA had been planning to explore beyond the solar system for the last ten years. The first ship to leave the solar system would go down in history. It was a big deal for anyone looking to make GASA their career.

June 21, 2169 0700 GMT

Preparations to study Venus were top priority. We had adjusted the ship's clocks to the Greenwich Mean Time (GMT) shortly after launch. A day on Venus lasts 223 days on earth so GASA figured that GMT would work as the best time measuring standard and it resembled earth time better. We lived on the Kennedy which remained in orbit. We used shuttles to visit the surface. For some unusual reason the atmosphere changed to where it was almost breathable, save a high amount of sulphur and another substance, T-5105. Captain Tanner issued the command that space suits and breathing equipment always be used regardless. He was protective of his new crew.

We were on Venus for a week without incident. We took soil samples, water samples, vegetation samples, and air quality. Most of our excursions were relatively boring but yielded very interesting data. Landing Teams consisted of no less than five people, with at least one bridge member, even if they're senior staff.

Jim Braddock and I were on the LRE (Long Range Exploration) team heading over to the far side of the planet. It was mid-morning when we discovered what looked like an ancient Greek temple. There were statues of vaguely familiar figures-not so much people we recognized but legends. One statue had a helmet and wings on his ankles; another female was adorned as if she were a queen, and so forth. In the middle of the temple was a device-much like a 21st century hospital pod but enclosed. As we moved closer to the device, we heard some clicking noises and a low hum. The Device then open up and above it appeared swirling lights and sounds. The light danced and swirled until it formed a humanoid female. The hum faded out and the figure began to speak:

"If you are seeing this message, it means that we have failed to return to the planet of our origin and that we have been dead many millennia. We are the last of a race that was the most advanced in the quadrant. We were charged to help the inhabitants of the next planet move forward and avoid the mistakes that brought our race to the edge of extinction. Our greed, our selfishness and our eventual disregard for basic humanity caused the ultimate destruction of all sentient life on this planet. When we realized it was too late to save our planet we reached out into the cosmos, sending out a few small consortia of the remaining leaders and elements of our technology, which we felt was the best hope for the survival of our culture, if not our race. The 3rd planet in this solar system was even more beautiful that our own. Our technology, social lessons and wisdom would live on and flourish on the 3rd planet. We were able to communicate with Venus for several years after the designated consortium arrived on the third planet, but there was trouble. Over time, the members of the consortium became self-important, arrogant to extent that they considered themselves god-like due to the exposure to the underdeveloped race of the 3rd planet. The primitive human race was easily dominated and, over time worshipped the members of the consortium. Zeus was the leader of our consortium and the commander of the vessel, Olympus. The beginning of our demise was when Zeus became drunk with power. The simplest of our technology was incomprehensible to those primitive people. Zeus established the consortium as gods and used the Olympus as their headquarters, knowing the primitive race would never enter or question where the consortium lived and kept their technology. Once we had established that the consortium was no longer following the charter of benevolence, they were ordered to return. They had found a chemical compound on the new planet that would have saved our world from the current plague but due to their arrogance they chose domination of an inferior world rather than saving their home planet. The plague had wiped out the male of our species years after the consortium had left so there was no way to continue our race. Artificial insemination methods proved unsuccessful due to the lack of the proper genetic material needed. One last effort culminated in mutating our genome structure but it came too late. Located in the base of this hologram projector is the last genetic material of our race, the last of the insemination serum. This device is programmed to execute an audio visual response. You understand my words because this device scanned your minds and adapted to your language. Also contained in this device is the planet's database, everything we could save that is the sum total of our world; all the cultures, everything we could save about our civilization. By now, you must have questions of us. Ask.

"Who are you?" I couldn't help myself. This was the single most amazing discovery in history.

"We are the Eleusians. My name is Venus."

"What were the names of the members of the consortium?"

These are the names of the Eleusian Consortium; each name is followed by their area of concern and some details we could derive from their communications after they arrived on the 3ʳᵈ planet:

Aphrodite

Arbitress of psychology and emotions. Her focus was on love, lust, and the effect of beauty in society. She was the wife of Hephaestus. It had been revealed the Ares became her lover. Eros is her son. She was considered the most beautiful of the Eleusian arbitresses. Her symbols are the scepter, myrtle, and dove.

Apollo

Arbiter of music, medicine, health, the arts, poetry, and archery. Also said to be the arbiter of light and truth. He is considered to be the most handsome of the arbiters. He is Artemis's twin brother, and son of Zeus. His symbols are the bow, lyre, and laurel.

Ares

Arbiter of war, murder and bloodshed. He was once a peaceful, loving man. He was supposed to teach the inhabitants how to avoid these but developed bloodlust and a desire to rule. He is brother to Athena, and is the son of Zeus. Had an affair with Aphrodite. His symbols are vultures, dogs, boars, and a spear.

Artemis

Arbitress of the hunt, wild things, and the moon. Purpose was to teach people to live off the land but not disrespect it. Protector of the young. She became associated with the moon. Apollo is her twin brother. Artemis is a virgin arbitress. Her symbols are the bow, dogs, and deer.

Athena

Arbitress of wisdom, warfare, strategy, handicrafts and reason. Her purpose was to show how to educate and think. Sister of Ares, and is the daughter of Zeus. She is the wisest of the arbiters. Her symbols are the aegis, owl, and olive tree.

Demeter

Arbitress of fertility, agriculture, grain and harvest. Her purpose was to teach agriculture. Demeter is a daughter of Cronus and Rhea and sister of Zeus. Her symbols are the scepter, torch, and corn.

Dionysus

Arbiter of entertainment, festivals, madness and merriment. His purpose was to show the value of diversions and entertainment. He represents not only the intoxicating power of wine, but also its social and beneficial influences. His symbols are the grape vine, ivy, and thyrsus. He is also an expert in psychology and psychiatry

Hades

Arbiter of death, commerce and wealth. His purpose was to train and guide the human race to conduct fair and balanced commerce. Brother of Poseidon, Zeus and Hera, and consort to Persephone. His symbols are the trident, the Helm of Darkness, and the three-headed dog, Cerberus.

Hephaestus

Arbiter of fire and the forge (arbiter of fire and smiths) with deformed legs. Once the Olympus was established as the center of power, Hephaestus was thrown off Mount Olympus as a baby by his mother and in some accounts by his father. He was able to set up a place to operate to do his appointed task. He makes armor for the arbiters and other heroes like Achilles. Son of Hera and Zeus is his father in some accounts. Married to Aphrodite, but she does not love him because he is deformed and, as a result, is cheating on him with Ares. He had a daughter named Pandora. His symbols are an axe, a hammer and a flame.

Hera

Arbitress of marriage, women, and childbirth. Her purpose was to teach women how to care for their children and to be help mates to men. Zeus' wife and sister. Appears with peacock feathers often. Her symbols are the scepter, diadem, and peacock.

Hermes

Arbiter of flight, criminal studies, and travelers. He assisted Hades
with commerce training. Messenger of the arbiters. He was the first
to abuse his power. His purpose was to educate people about the
effects of criminal activity in society. He likes to trick people and is
very inventive. Hermes invented the lyre using a turtle shell and
sinew. His symbols are the caduceus and winged boots.

Hestia

Arbitress of the hearth and home, the focal point of every household.
Daughter of Rhea and Cronus. Gave up her seat as one of the Twelve
Olympians to tend to the sacred flame on Mount Olympus for
Dionysus. Her symbol is the hearth.

Poseidon

Poseidon Arbiter of the sea. He created horses from sea foam. Arbiter
of earthquakes as well. Also called 'Earth Shaker' and 'Storm Bringer'.
His symbols are horses, sea foam, dolphins, and a trident.

Zeus

The king of the arbiters, the commander of the Olympus and the
arbiter of the sky and thunder. His symbols are the thunderbolt, eagle,
bull, and oak tree.

We were stunned. Here we have just discovered not only that the
ancient Greek gods of mythology were real beings, also that they
were aliens with the mission to make life better on earth. So much of
our human history was validated in a few minutes. Knowledge and
information that was secret, lost for centuries was all of a sudden in
the palm of our hands. We called the other teams to investigate the
pod and the area around it. Once Venus was done speaking she gave
us instructions on how to operate and retrieve the serum.
Unfortunately, time had damaged the containment system in the pod
and there was a small explosion. There was minimal damage but the
area filled with a gas that seemed to linger and permeate everything
within a 10-meter radius. Also, the serum must have mutated and

when we tried to extract it. Since there was an atmosphere here, had our helmets off and were unprotected. That proved unfortunate for all of us. According to Venus, the serum originally was supposed to balance the hormones between men and women. This would make them more sympathetic and understanding to one another. The mutation caused an imbalance in the hormonal structure and gradually began to alter the hormones and DNA of an exposed person. The process was gradual so we didn't see the effects for days.

June 28, 2169 1422 Hours

Another week went by while we analyzed the data from the pod. Mankind had come so far but nothing like the Eleusians. Propulsion, sustainable energy, medical advances and more were entered into our computers. Troy came into sickbay and complained of some unusual pain.
"How long have you been having it?"
"About a day. My chest feels tight."
"Were you working out in the fitness center?"
"No, I had too much work to do. All that data is too fantastic. These Eleusians could move objects just by thinking about it! We haven't scratched a tenth of data they left. We're still loading it into the computer."
"That's incredible!"
"Yeah it is. -" Troy's voice trailed off as he started to faint. "Troy!" I yelled. "Orderly! Get in here!" Two medics ran in and propped Troy up. Get him into a bed!"
The medics moved Troy over to a gurney and wheeled him down the hall to the first bed. I followed them, very alarmed that Troy had fainted. As soon as he was on the bed, I began a medi-scan. He was stable but unconscious. The scan also showed that he lost fifteen pounds in a relatively short time. 'Supplements?' I thought, but set it aside. Right now his heart rate was very high so I administered the energy hypo to bring it down. We still had chemical compounds, drugs they used to call them, but since the Martian Colony discovery we were able to replace most drugs with directed energy. The Martians had discovered that with the right amount of energy and at the right frequency, organic cells can respond in specific ways. We

have in essence cured cancer, Alzheimer's, ALS, IFA, and the common cold.

Troy's heart rate started to drop. I breathed easier and released the orderlies. "Thanks, guys. I'll call if I need you again." Once Troy was back in the safe zone, I administered a sedative to allow his body to rest. I figured an hour should do it. I went to my desk and recorded the incident. As I left sickbay to inform the captain and get some coffee, I decided to add a genetic rover to the medi-scan. That would detect any change at the genetic level. I put a blanket over Troy and headed toward the bridge.

I passed some of the other team members that went to the temple. I noticed they seemed a little different. I passed it off as fatigue and rode the lift to the bridge. "Where's the Captain?"

"In his call room, Sir." An ambitious crewman spoke up.

"Thanks. And please call me Doctor."

"Yes, Doctor." The crewman smiled and relaxed. I strode into the large conference room off to the side of the bridge. The Captain was sitting at his desk eating lunch. "What can I do for you doctor?"

"Just needed to report that the First Officer is in sickbay."

"What's wrong with him?"

"He came in complaining of some mild chest pain. Then he passed out in my arms."

"Is he okay?"

"He has a slight fever, but I am running a medi-scan on him now. It doesn't seem serious, but I included a genetic rover to be safe."

"Okay. Keep me posted. I will stop by sickbay in a little while."

"Roger that, Sir."

I left the commander's office and heading back to sickbay to check on Troy. Again I got that uneasy feeling. People seem to be different. Mostly the men. I arrived back at sickbay to check on Troy. He was still unconscious but he seemed thinner. He wasn't a large man but he had a medium build. Now it seemed smaller and his hair was longer. It was very strange. I checked the scan and it was very unusual. His DNA has been altered. Chromosomes are in a state of flux and his skin started to turn pink. His heart rate had lowered but it wasn't back to normal. I decided not to give him any other pulse lowering treatment. I decided to stay past my shift just to be safe.

Troy was stable so set a medi-alert through my pad and retired for the evening.

Chapter 2

THE GREAT CONVERSION

JUNE 30, 2169 0615 Hours

I woke up a little early. It was my parents' 65th wedding anniversary and I wanted to wish them a happy one. Dad loves to travel so I prepaid for a weekend getaway in Hawaii. They love to go there and reminisce about their honeymoon. I have a married younger brother who is an actor. He was the creative one while I was more practical, the logical one. I knew I wanted to be a doctor when I patched him up when he fell off a roof. He was playing Romeo and Juliet. He thought it humorous and true to Shakespeare for him to play Juliet. His holographic generator-his Romeo, malfunctioned mid scene and when he went down to fix it, he slipped and fell, breaking his leg. I set it after studying anatomy and first aid in middle school. After a stern lecture from my father at the hospital, the attending physician pulled me aside and said it was a textbook set. He said that if he didn't know better, he would have thought a doctor had set it. I was on cloud nine for weeks.

After I sent the message, I was feeling a little queasy. I looked in the mirror and notice my face looked thinner. I also felt a tightness in my chest. My hair felt thicker and slightly longer. I sense that whatever Troy had now I had it too. I heard some groaning outside my cabin door. I look around and everyone seemed to suffering the same symptoms. I ran to sick bay to see Troy. In the bed where I left him the night before was a woman, bearing a strong resemblance to Troy. She was awake and gestured toward me. "Doc, what happened to me?" she said with some difficulty.

"Troy?" I said.

She nodded. "I feel weird. Better but weird." Troy was still pretty weak.

"I don't know. You were the first with these symptoms but now it seems everyone has them. Including me."

"Yeah. Your hair." It seemed to be growing. It was even longer than it was when I got up. "Do you remember anything?"

"I remember last night coming in, chest hurt, talking to you and then- I think I passed out."

"That's it. Do you remember what happened before you came to see me? Anything unusual?

"We were downloading the data from the pod. It was going okay. Then-", his voice trailed off as he was passing out again.

"Then what? Burst of light, plasma. Filled the room but no one was hurt. At least I don't think so."

"Okay-rest now. Once you're strong enough we'll do another medi-scan."

Troy nodded and fell back to sleep. I had a bona fide, medical mystery on my hands and if I don't figure out what's going on the entire crew will be in jeopardy. I had to see the Captain.

I ran to the lift and used the executive express command. It took me straight to the bridge, non-stop. I burst onto the bridge screaming for the Captain. The bridge crew had been afflicted too, but for some reason about half were totaling changed to women and the Captain was barely recognizable. He appeared to be 75% converted to female.

"Captain! Are you okay?"

"No, cannot stay awake, you must initiate the Sentry Protocol!" The Captain repeated 'Sentry" as he lost consciousness. My blood was burning but I still seemed to be able to function. I suspected that I, too would pass out at some point but my "conversion" seemed to be a slower rate. I sat in the command chair and pulled out my pad. I tapped in my security code and inserted the pad into the command slot, located on the chair's console. The computer asked for my retinal scan and then the lancet for the blood confirmation came out. I swiped my finger across the lancet and the computer paused. It never pauses with retinal and blood confirmation. "Computer, why is there a delay?"

"DNA scan is incomplete."

"Why?"

"DNA is corrupted. Closest match is Dr. Darius Obama. Chief Medical Officer"

"Override! I am Obama."

"Voice print corrupted. Closest match is-"

"DEPLOY THE SENTRY! NOW!"

"DNA, retinal scan sufficient to engage Sentry. Deploying Sentry on your command."

"Deploy Sentry now!"

Activating the Sentry Protocol was more draining than I expected. I tapped the ship-wide com and made the announcement. "This is Chief Medical Officer Obama. By now many of you are aware that an unknown illness has infected many of the Kennedy crewmembers. I am also affected but not completely debilitated by the sickness. I have activated the Sentry Protocol which sets the ship back on an automatic, emergency course back to Earth. We will enter the highest orbit around Earth and remain quarantined until a treatment or cure can be found. Until then, I call for anyone unaffected by this unknown illness to report to the bridge immediately. That is all."

The announcement also drained me. I felt weak but had to save enough energy to get to sickbay to try and figure out what is going on with us. I wanted an unaffected crew member on the bridge to monitor our trip home. They would not have control unless the Sentry is released and any of the bridge crew can do that as long as I add my authorization. The lift came back and three crewmembers stepped off. All women.

"How are you three feeling?"

The first crew member spoke up. "We're all fine sir. As a matter of fact none of the female crew were affected, at least not yet."

"What your name?"

"Ensign Morrison, Sir. Quantum Physics department." She was tall and well built. She looked like command material."

"Chief Petty Officer Williams. Engineering."

"And you?"

"Ensign Lattimore." Physics Lab"

"Okay, until further notice Ensign Morrison is in command. Williams, you are chief engineer and Lattimore you are science officer and first mate. Are there anymore unaffected that you know of?"

Morrison spoke up. "Sir, we've noticed that none of the other female crew are affected."

"How many?"

"In total, about seven. The rest should be here shortly."

"All right, Commander, when they get here, assign them as appropriately as you can. I am returning to sickbay to see if I can figure this thing out."

"Yes sir!"

I staggered to the lift and headed to sickbay. By the time I got there, all the beds were taken so I thought I would rest for a short time before trying to work. I got to my quarters and passed out onto the bed. It was noontime.

July 1, 2169, 1505 Two Hours Before Entering Earth Orbit.

I rolled over, half asleep and saw a blurry figure standing next to my bed. The figure was tall and dark haired. It was Ensign Morrison and she was checking on me. "Sir! Sir! You've been asleep for over 24 hours. Are you okay?"

I sat up and rubbed my eyes. I had an abundance of hair that fell down onto my shoulders. I stood up and immediately sat back down. I felt better but very different. I felt smaller and misshapen. My hips were much wider and my genitals were not right. My feet were half the size they were before. I was a female and I have no idea how it happened. Morrison helped me stand. "You recognized me. I must look completely different."

"Actually sir, we've been monitoring the executive staff and bridge crew. Both with DNA scanning and visual recording to document the changes. You look more like a female member of your family. You have regenerated nine-tenths of your tissue so you should feel younger than you did before."

"Amazing. Let me see a mirror."

Morrison held a mirror up to me and I took it. "I look like my mother at about 25 years old."

"How old are you actually, sir?"

"I'm 37. And call me doctor. 'Sir' isn't going to work for a while, at least until I reverse this."

"Yes, Doctor."

"How is everyone else?"

"Well, so far, the majority of the male crew has changed gender. None of us are qualified to give a full medical examination so we came to you first."

"Smart. Okay let me walk around a bit. This body is balanced differently."

Morrison offered some unusual advice. "Try walking on the balls of your feet at first. That should help regain your natural balance. We can fabricate new shoes for you when you want."

"Thanks. Let me check Troy. He was almost changed before I went up to the bridge yesterday." The trio went to sick bay and saw him/her. "Troy?"

"So to speak. Not much of the man I was left." He was right. Laying on the bed was a stunningly beautiful woman, with a slight resemblance to the First Mate. "I felt fine yesterday, though I was puzzled and scared because I was no longer a man. I figured I'd better stay put until I heard from you. Then I heard the announcement you made and didn't know what to do."

"It's unprecedented to say the least." I was still getting used to my higher voice. I heard my mom when I spoke. "I'll need some of the females, natural ones, to do some tests. If we can identify some anomalies we may find an answer." Morrison you will continue to command."

"Ah, Doctor? We have a slight problem."

"What is it?"

"Commander Tanner wants to resume command. He, well she, insists."

"Where is he, sorry-she now?"

"On the bridge. She's waiting for me to transfer command back and shut down the Sentry."

"Under no circumstances are you to relinquish command until I say so. We have no idea what's happening or how it will continue to affect us. We can't even leave the ship when we get back to Earth."

"Yes Sir." Morrison turned sharply and marched back towards the lift. I was surprised at Tanner that he would be that stubborn. We have a ship full of men who have inexplicably turned into women. He should have stayed in his quarters. I released Troy as long as he, (nuts!), she felt up to duty. I felt surprisingly good too. I suspect that once the change has completed there were positive side effects. Tanner is probably feeling that way too. I stepped on the bridge. "Captain Tanner," I said in an increasingly husky and appealing voice, "What the hell are you doing?"

"I beg your pardon, Doctor?" A stunning, statuesque blond with hair down to the center of her back turned around. I almost didn't recognize him/her. "You are not ready to command, yet."

"I feel fine, Darius. Even better than I did as a man. I feel 10 years younger."

"I know. So do I but we have to make sure there is no apparent threat."

"I don't see any threat, Doctor. Yes-it is a very weird situation but no one has died, right?"

"So far. I'm actually not sure. I need to examine over 200 people. Including you."

"Alright Doctor, alright. Ensign, you have the conn."

"Aye, Sir, sorry, Ma'am."

"Pronoun trouble," I said. "We'll work it out."

Tanner and I walked to the lift and went to sickbay. I performed a full medi-scan on him/her and analyzed the results. "What's the result, Doc?"

"Well, according to all the tests I've performed, you are a perfectly healthy, 30 year old woman."

"I'm not sure that's what I wanted to hear."

"Well the scans on myself and Troy say the same. The question is how did we switch gender and why?"

"We'll be in space dock in about an hour."

"I don't think I have the answer by then. The female crew members were not affected. So that's a start."

"A start? How do you mean?"

"Whatever changed us only affected the males. So something about our male anatomy must have triggered the process."

"It has to be connected to the Venus pod and that data."

"Agreed. I will talk to Troy and see what he, she has come up with. For now, we'll have to leave the command of the ship in Morrison's hands."

"How is she doing?"

"She is capable and I think she is doing fine. She'll command her own ship sooner than later."

"I agree." Tanner stopped to ponder her next sentence. "I just hope I can get it back."

At that point I wasn't sure if Tanner was making a joke or if she was actually concerned. I think I may have seen a tear in her eye. I decided to ignore my thought and get the research underway.

The first concern was the crew and their welfare. I went to the science lab to meet up with Troy. She had recovered fully except for the gender change and was working to analyze the Eleusian data and the alien pod. She was slightly shorter than before-medium build, attractive figure, and shoulder length honey brown hair.

"Troy! How are you feeling?"

"Fantastic. Once I woke up yesterday I felt great. How are you?"

"Still getting used to my new anatomy. Any progress on the data?" I was hoping for some good news.

"Well we just finished the download. It's fascinating-we aren't even a tenth of the way through the data and there is technology we haven't even dreamed of. The thing is it's written in Latin. That's actually good because it's easily translated."

"Can you filter it for medical and biological information? We need to figure out what happen to us." I was hopeful that the cause of this epidemic may also hold the cure.

"Yeah I think we can pull that out. Give me about an hour."

"We'll be in Earth orbit by then."

"Okay."

I went back to sick bay and monitored the medi-scans of the crew. It would take another day or two complete them and analyze the new information. I had 3 stations going at once and the orderlies, who were the first ones scanned, continued to work.

As I looked at the monitor, the genetic information from the scans were collating. It would take another couple of hours to have enough data to analyze. "This is frustrating." Jakob, my senior med-tech, said, exasperated. "All this hair keeps getting in my way."

"Tie it up."

"Everyone's doing that. I can't find any bands."

"I have a couple.""

"Thanks."

"No problem. How are you feeling, Jake?"

"Other than being female, I feel fine. Great even. But I feel something else. It's mild but noticeable."

"What is it?"

"I have-urges.

"What kind of urges?"

"Sexual. I want a man."

"Is this normal?"

"You mean was I a gay man before? No. I'm straight. I was even seeing somebody casually on earth."

"Do we have any gay crew members? I mean they're not required to disclose it if they are."

"I'm sure we do but I don't know who they are."

"Okay. Quietly find out. Also find anyone who's transgender too. They might need special medical attention."

"Right." Jake needed to focus on something else. He was with me at the base hospital so we've known each other a few years. I recommended him for this post and I have not regretted it. All of a sudden I felt flush. It was a strange sensation, unfamiliar and a little unsettling. I shook it off and went to Tanner's quarters.

"How are you, Commander?"

"Adjusting. I'm glad these uniforms are programmable. I had to add support in the chest region."

"Right I didn't think of that. I could send out an upgrade to the suits."

"Not yet. Let folks do it on their own. More comfortable."

"Okay. Have you been feeling well otherwise?"

"Yes. Excellent in fact. Except every so often I get a mild headache. Not bad, just comes and goes."

"Hmm. Maybe a delayed reaction to the change? I'll send up a pain reliever."

"Thanks."

"Let me know if you experience anything else."

"You bet. Now, about the quarantine. It seems we are stuck here until we can figure out what this thing is. Have you made any progress."

"Not much. Whatever it is, it only turns men into women."

"We know that."

"Right but, female crewmembers are still female and seem unaffected."

"I understand. So the females need not be quarantined."

"It seems like it but I am still running tests. We're pulling the biological data from the alien pod. I'm hoping it will provide some answers."

"I hope so. I really want this over. Keep me posted."

"Me too. I will check in later."

I heard my own voice say I wanted this to end, but I wasn't fully convinced. I felt better than I have in a long time. I'm only 37, but I feel like a teenager. I decided to do some personal tests on my new body. I changed into workout clothes and headed down to the fitness center. I was a fair runner, so I thought I would start there. I run a mile in about 8 minutes. I set the time and started on a moderate pace and I felt lighter and stronger than normal. I picked up the pace and soon I was running full speed. I ran for a full 10 minutes and checked the treadmill and saw that I did 4.5 miles! I couldn't believe it. I decided to try weight lifting. I can lift about 200 pounds. Women typically have less muscle mass than men, even women in top physical condition. I decided to start light. First I set the machine for 80 pounds and did about 200 reps fast. Then I raised it to 100, then 150, then 200 then 250 and finally 300 pounds. I probably could have gone higher but I was just flabbergasted. I did 200 reps each time and ran more than double the distance I normally could! I had to report this to the captain. First I ran (because I still could) back to sickbay. I reconfigured the medi-scan to check adrenaline, muscle composition and dopamine levels. I had the entire crew's initial medi-scans from when we were preparing for the mission. I pulled up my scan and stats and began a cellular comparison. Jake was back in the lab analyzing the first batch of scans. "Jake! See if you can do a cellular comparison. I think I've found something!" I was excited but neither winded not fatigued from my workout. I moved to the ship's com and called Tanner. "Captain, please report to sick bay."

Tanner seemed to appear out of thin air. She was wearing a revealing outfit that was uncharacteristic for the situation. I ignored it due to the importance of my findings. "Look at this!"

"What am I looking at, Doctor?"

"This is my medi-scan just before we left Earth. This second scan I just did half an hour ago. My new, female body is pumping out ten times the amount of adrenaline, insulin, dopamine and muscle strength that our male bodies did. The levels vary slightly with each person, depending on build, genetic history and body chemistry, but in all cases we are better physical specimens than we were as men."

"That's incredible! No wonder I've been able to think faster and clearer. But one question? Why did it change our gender? Why did it only affect the men and not the women?"

"We still don't know, but maybe we can speculate as to why. It is possible that the Eleusians were experimenting with genetic manipulation. Change would happen faster in a female specimen since there are more biochemical operations in a female due to their ability to procreate. Much like a computer, it looked for an appropriate chemical combination and altered it."

"Is it reversible?"

"I still don't know, but that bears another question."

"What's that?"

"Would we want to? It's almost like we've found the fountain of youth with gender change the one major difference."

"You mean price. The price of giving up of our male gender in return to be superwomen."

"I guess that's a way of looking at it."

"I'm not sure it's a price I want to pay."

"Let's hope we have the option."

Chapter 3

THE ADJUSTMENT

July 21, 2169 0800 Hours

Three weeks have passed since the Venus Mission. We have
downloaded all the data from the alien vessel and we are about 35%
through the analysis. We have found cures for cancer, birth defects
and dementia. We found technological advances that dwarf anything
discovered by man thus far. The only thing we have not found is a
way to reverse the gender change. Oddly enough, no one seems
bothered by it. I suspect that included in the compound that changed
us was the ability to accept the change. The other odd thing is that all
that were changed were heterosexual. Even the gay crew members
that were changed from male to female remained attracted to men.
Let it stand in my personal record that there was no duress,
harassment or force used against the homosexual crewmembers. This
is confirmed by their attached sworn statements. We want to make
sure that regardless of anyone's personal feelings about the subject,
the ship's gay population was and is treated fairly and without
oppression of any kind.
The ship's quarantine is still in effect and the female command crew
is performing admirably. Ensign Morrison has been promoted to
Lieutenant as well as the rest of the command staff. I had just run 23
miles in the fitness center and then showered. I headed over to the
data lab to see the latest developments. I met Jim Braddock the
science officer who was in charge of the lab. "What's the latest, Jim?"
"I may have found a clue about the change. It seems that the
Eleusians were planning to return to Earth after about 1000 years.
They had extremely long life spans. Before they went back to Earth
but there seemed to be something of a negative political action that
halted it."
"You mean a war?"
"No, more like a coup. Several of the gods or arbiters or whatever,

wanted to colonize Earth, and some wanted to just educate us and then leave. Some wanted to travel throughout the solar system."

"That may explain what happened to the Martians. It was by sheer dumb luck that we found any evidence of their civilization."

"Right. Well according to their records, the chief arbiter, Zeus, ordered that all the data, chemical compounds and records be-there doesn't seem to be an English word for it so I will say scanned-into the alien pod which isn't really a pod as it is a neural database."

"Amazing."

"There's more. There was only one of these pods, with a few of these drives in it. I think it's safe to assume that there was an impending disaster."

"What kind of disaster?"

"Hard to tell. It wasn't a planet killer because well, because everything we found was intact. Some of them may have left the planet for deep space. Others may have settled quietly on Earth. There's evidence of both." Jim flipped her hair up and I noticed that she was wearing makeup. I chose not to say anything but this isn't the first expression of femininity that I've seen. Other crew members have dressed up and even went on night's out. Tanner has not said anything and she may be suffering the same issues. I made a mental note to see her later and looked around the lab further. "Jim-"

"Jaime, actually. I'm going by Jaime these days."

"Okay. Jaime, any more medical data?"

"Yes, over here. I put it into a drive unit. You can take it with you. Be advised though it's' pretty full and that may not be all of it."

"Thanks, Jaime. I will see you later."

The drive unit was the size of a large suitcase. Fortunately, it was on wheels so I dragged it back to sickbay. I realized I hadn't showered so I left the unit at my desk and went into my quarters. I felt like a long shower and had a desire for perfumed soap and other girly shower things. My beard didn't grow anymore and the hair on my legs was pretty fine. I decided to put on some casual clothes and head back to my desk. I set the protocols on the computer with gender change and oddly it came up with nothing except a binary code. I switched to genetic data. This looked promising, as it came up with tons of data and video. It was in Latin and mine was pretty rusty. I ran a translation app and it was all readable. It was about 800 pages and hundreds of videos. I started at the beginning. The first video showed what I took as a laboratory, though it was an odd design. It was a strange Greco-Roman style with unfamiliar technology. I played it.

"I am Apollo. I have been charged with developing the insemination serum to save our dying race. Here I have documented the chemical compound, received from the third planet."

Apollo continued with several molecular series, elements both familiar and alien and finally after 6 hours he found the proper sequence. He tested it on an earth woman they had brought back and found that it worked with no ill effects to the subject. He recorded 4 more video of tests which were somewhat progressive but uneventful. Unfortunately, in the fifth video, Apollo faced another problem.

"It has been 5 months since the first test. We have tested the serum on Eleusian, 3rd and 4th planet subjects. The 4th planet subjects reject the serum completely. I am sorry to say it was lethal to them. I have petitioned the consortium to give restitution to the subject's family. If I had any idea that the serum would have been lethal, I never would have used it." Apollo seemed genuinely remorseful about the death of the Martian. It was several weeks (I guess-that may be hours in Venus time) before he made another video.

"The serum had not worked as well as we hoped. The 3rd planet subject seems to have fared the best with one major flaw: all infants are female. They are healthy, even enhanced with greater musculature, adrenal processes and dopamine production. The serum was based on a Meltaxion steroid which was programmable at the molecular level. The effect, however, has caused the serum to only produce females. We knew that the 3rd planet had an abundance of males and females. We discovered that after testing on an island of natives, the serum rewrote their cells and turned them female. Xenometer, the science officer and commander of the vessel, Valon, was tasked to test the inhabitants of the island with the serum. He tested the humans and discovered that the serum has a viral effect and there is no known antidote. The male subjects underwent a metamorphosis and became female. Their bodies were enhanced and improved, due to the Meltaxion molecular programming. The viral effect was brought about the Valon and they were all changed. The sad result is that they could never come home again. They were stranded on that island and decided to never leave. They salvaged the

Valon and used the technology to survive and cloak the island from the rest of the planet's inhabitants."

I paused the video. This was unprecedented. We have learned more about our own planet that scholars and scientist have for the past 6000 years. We also have an explanation as to what happened to us. Another sobering thought: can we ever return to Earth? Will this gender-altering serum doom earth to extinction? I called the captain. "You need to get down here."

"I'm on my way." Tanner knows my serious tone so when she hears it he doesn't question me until we're together. I continued to view the videos. The consortium was able to isolate the effects of serum but they did not find a way to reverse it. "Maybe some of the other videos can provide answers as to why they didn't find the antidote." I thought. "With all this advanced knowledge I find it hard to believe they couldn't fix it." Tanner came in. She was wearing a cocktail dress and heels. My fears of the captain giving in to his feminine side were pretty much confirmed. "You aren't going to believe me."

"Try me." I detected a slight giggle. It chilled me.

"The Eleusians created a fertility serum because their race was dying out."

"You're kidding me." I heard the seriousness of the old Tanner returning.

"This drive unit has the first batch of medical data and it is chock full of answers."

"And more questions, I'll bet." Tanner moved in closer any I could smell her perfume. I felt a little manly enjoying her smell. Then it dawned on me. "Computer, show pheromone levels in the room." The computer beeped and responded, "The level of pheromones in the room is 68%"

"Is that high?" Tanner giggled again.

"Extremely. Computer show same for the whole ship." The computer beeped again, although it took more time for analysis. "The level of pheromones on the ship is 324%."

"Oh my God. If there were any normal men on this ship, they'd be out of their minds."

"I wish there were men on the ship." Tanner said, again giggling.

"Are you okay?"

"Well, I don't feel bad, but very different. I want certain things, things that I never thought about as a man. I had a bubble bath last

night. I haven't a bubble bath since I was little boy. Plus I have thoughts and feelings that are completely different but yet familiar."
I had to admit to myself that I felt the same way. I tried on several different outfits this morning before I went to the fitness center. I was actually concerned with the way I looked! Tanner started to bite her lower lip. "What's wrong?"
"I don't think I want to change back. I like being this way and it's scaring me."
"I understand. I feel the same way but our first priority is the safety of the crew and the planet. This serum marooned the last ship that transported it and we are in the same situation. If we try to go back to our lives on Earth, we could easily doom the planet and the human race itself. The genetic pool has been contaminated and I don't know if I can fix it." I felt myself starting to cry. It shocked me and I shook it off. Tanner uncharacteristically hugged and comforted me. "It's going to be okay. You are the best doctor in GASA. That's why I picked you."
"Thanks, Commander."
"You've been at this a while. Why don't you take a break? It's almost dinner time. You should change."
"Maybe you're right. I'll take a fresh crack at it in the morning."
I went to my quarters and put on some casual clothes. I didn't feel any better so I had the replicator make some different clothes. I tried some of the casual clothes I wore as a man. Now that I am a woman they just didn't feel right. So I started experimenting with different looks and eventually I found a nice dress. My brain was now fully female and in a surreal way, it was almost like I was getting ready for a date. I had urges, not sexual ones but, a desire to look.... pretty. I wanted to wear make-up and after a while I was mincing around my quarters. Whatever male part of me was left was riding around in my head like a passenger. The female was driving and she was in full force. Once I was satisfied with my look, I called Tanner. "Are you ready?"
"I've been ready for an hour and a half! What are you doing there?"
"You'll see!" I said with a giggle. I've never giggled in my life. I went down to the cantina and met Tanner. The mess staff turned the cantina into a dance club and half the ship's crew seemed to be there. People were dancing and enjoying themselves. "The crew needed

this." Tanner said.

"I think you're right. We've been cooped up on this ship longer than planned and everyone definitely needed to blow off some steam."

"That includes us, too! Let's dance!" Tanner grabbed my wrist and pulled me onto the dance floor. Whatever male inhibitions we had evaporated on the dance floor. What was actually a relief that the crew, despite all the weird stuff that's happened, has adapted pretty well. I think it was a smart idea to have crew that had no attachments, no family. It especially came in handy due to what happened next.

July 22, 2169, 0730 Hours

It's customary to indulge heavily in alcohol during a military social event. On many occasions I've questioned where I woke up simply because I didn't remember how I got there. These new enhanced female bodies apparently can party as well as they can perform physically. I turned in about 3am and woke up at 7am and I felt rested with no hangover. I was still in my dress and my make-up had faded. I wash my face and changed into my new, modified uniform. I felt hungry which was weird because I hadn't felt hungry in a few days. As a matter of fact, I don't remember the last time I ate. I went to the dining hall (the cantina was next to it) and got breakfast. It was busy and everyone had a large quantity of food on their plate. I ordered my eggs and fruit and sat down. Tanner moved over to me and Morrison came over, too. "How's the command crew, Lieutenant?"

"Fine, Sir-Ma' am."

"Ma'am will suffice. We will have to get used to the fact that we'll be this way for the time being. Doc, any progress on an antidote?"

"Not yet. We do know now that the Eleusians knew an antidote had to be created. With some of their beginning calculations I may have something viable in about six months."

"Six months!"

"Yes. Even with their advanced technology, we are months away from any kind of chemical compound."

"Okay." Tanner finished her food and said, "Lieutenant Morrison, meet me in the conference room in about an hour."

"Yes, Ma'am."

"Talk to you later, Doctor."

"Aye, Sir." Tanner walked off, in the way a ship's commander does. I looked at Morrison and she looked concerned. "Don't worry," I consoled her. "I'm sure it's just a routine meeting."

"Thanks, Doctor. I appreciate it." Morrison got up and returned her tray. I was a little nervous myself but turned my attention to finding the antidote. I walked back to sick bay and continued sifting through the data. Two hours passed and the com clicked on. "Doctor, may I see you in the conference room?"

"On my way." I needed a break though I could have kept going. Mental acuity is another blessing that comes with being an enhanced female. "Reporting as ordered, Ma'am."

"Come in. I have received a change of orders from GASA."

"Oh?"

"Yes. They want us to go to the Mars Colony."

"Why?"

"Well, since we can't risk endangering the Earth with this virus we have, they will resupply us there. They are sending supplies there and evacuating the area so to prevent contamination."

"I see, well it beats staying here. I think most of the crew wanted to go home and being this close without letting them off the ship is torture."

"I agree. That's why I asked for the next assignment."

"Okay and that would be?"

"Deep space exploration."

"Is the Kennedy adapted for deep space?"

"It will be on Mars. The only problem is that our engineers will need to do the upgrades."

"That will take almost a year! You accepted this?"

"Yes, Doctor. I also made arrangements to take back command of the Kennedy."

"That's why you met with Morrison."

"Yes, most of the bridge crew has been rotated back into their previous positions. Morrison has had a taste of command so I wanted to do this gradually. She will remain as second officer, unless Troy wants to let her be first. Jaime will continue to oversee the pod operations and assist you on finding an antidote. I plan to be back in command as of August 1."

"I see. Okay. I admire the way you are making the change gradual."

"Well it's only fair. Morrison's done an excellent job and it would be demoralizing to just yank her out. As soon as we get to Mars, I am going to recommend her for command of her own ship. She may want to take some of the current bridge crew so the timing is good."

"Very good, Ma'am. Anything else?"

"Actually, yes. I have decided that once we can contain the virus, I will probably remain a woman."

"Oh?" I was not surprised.

"The truth is that I like it." Tanner seemed to be happier as a woman. "I never would have considered it as a man. But now, I can't see myself as anything else as female."

"I understand." I really did.

"What about you?"

"I haven't decided yet. I mean it's not unpleasant being a female, especially and enhanced one. We should probably give the crew the option."

"That's the best thing to do. I have heard others saying the same thing."

"We will put that into consideration as we find the antidote."

"Keep me posted."

"Roger that, Ma'am."

I thought about remaining a woman, but I still have my parents to consider. I'm not sure how they'd react if their eldest son became their daughter. Lots to ponder.

July 25, 2169 1130 Hours

Most of the bridge crew was back to posts, with their alternates still working side by side half of the duty day. Tanner was back in command from noon to 6pm with Morrison in command 6am to noon. She seemed to adjust to co-commanding and even learning more. We finished analyzing the third drive unit from the alien pod and made a major breakthrough. Finally, we found the genome sequence of the serum. We then were able to develop a counter-sequence but there was a problem. Tanner came down immediately when I told him we were close. "So what's the problem?"

"We need a male to test it. We need to expose him to the serum, then see if the antidote will change him back."

"I'm not sure GASA with get on board with that. Why can't we use a volunteer that used to be a man?"

I paused for a very long time. I didn't know how to tell him that we have been women too long. I took a breath. "The genome sequencing takes a short time to work but a few weeks to lock the chromosomes into the new, female order. Had we found the information earlier, we could have changed back. Now we are women forever whether we want to be or not."

"Hmm. Well that may not be as much as a problem as you think. I have been informally surveying the crew and most aren't concerned with being men again."

"Right but those who want to change back, can't. That's the bad news."

"There's good news?"

"Yes. For us, the antidote also acts as a vaccine. The good news is that we can inoculate ourselves and return to earth."

"Amazing work, Doctor. We will have an event in the cantina tonight. That way we can share the good and bad news with everyone."

"We'll need to set up vaccination stations. Once we get everyone immunized they can go ashore and break it to their families." I thought that was very compassionate of Tanner. Her demeanor is much softer than before. She is still a great commander.

July 29, 2169 1745 Hours

"This is Captain Tanner. In 15 minutes, all off duty personnel will report to the cantina. There will be an awards ceremony and then an update on our current and next mission. That is all." I am wondering how the crew is going to react to the news that they are stuck as women. I hadn't decided whether or not I was going to change back and now there was no option. The good news is that we could at least go home to earth. I think that for most, that would be the most desirable option. Since the change, no one has been sick or even suffered a serious injury. We are not indestructible-a crew member suffered a second degree plasma burn but not serious. She was fine in a few days. Our healing properties and immune systems were off the charts. It's actually the best qualified crew to go into deep space. Tanner had informed GASA central that we had found a vaccine/antidote. They released us from quarantine as soon as everyone was vaccinated. They sent some custom supplies to space dock to be loaded on the Kennedy. The rest of the supplies we needed were already on Mars and we are still slated to make a stop, though it will be much shorter than originally anticipated. The new deep space upgrades can be done in a few weeks but multiple crews rather than our crew taking a year. All in all, things were looking good.

I heard Tanner's announcement as I got out of the shower. I put on my dress uniform (modified, of course) and headed toward the cantina. Troy joined me halfway. "So we're still going to Mars?"

"Yes. The good news is that we won't be there as long as originally planned."

"That's great. Now I have to find time to tell my mom that her son is now her daughter."

"GASA will have counselors to help you. Don't worry."

"Thanks, Doc."

We arrived at the cantina and I went up on the small stage next to Tanner. She was in dress uniform and full make-up. She's gotten pretty good with it and looked like a model. Once everyone was settled, she stood and walked to the lectern. "Ladies, welcome to the first USS Kennedy Awards Ceremony. A few months ago, we started mankind's greatest mission, traveling into the unknown reaches of space. That curiosity changed all of us. I take full responsibility for your situation. For those of you who did not want to remain women, I am truly sorry. I have made arrangements with GASA to assist you in any way that you wish. You may choose to leave the service, but I hope that you don't. This is the finest crew in the fleet and I would travel the stars with each and every one of you, any time." The crowd exploded in applause. Once it died down, the captain continued. "The good news is that we are no longer quarantined. Doctor Obama and her team worked extremely hard and put in long hours to get back as much of our life as possible. Well done, Doctor." Another round of raucous applause erupted. "We have some happy business to attend to so let's get to it."

Tanner announced the names of twenty people, from the kitchen staff up to engineering. He then called the bridge crew and then finally Lieutenant Morrison. "For diligence above and beyond the call of duty, I present the Silver Star to Lieutenant Vivian Morrison, for interim command of the USS Kennedy. Your hard work and leadership was exemplary." She hung the medal around Morrison's neck and hugged her. Morrison smiled and stood to the side while Tanner regained control. "I have another announcement. I have recommended Lt. Morrison for command. The USS Vonnegut is in need of a skipper and it's a fine ship." Tanner turned to Morrison, "It's yours if you want it. You can even take your bridge crew you had from the Kennedy if you want to."

"Wow, thank you, Ma'am."

"My pleasure. Now on to new business. As I said earlier, we are still going to Mars for resupply and a ship wide upgrade for deep space. The Vonnegut is to be upgraded 6 months after us so Morrison, we'll see you out there. Right now we are getting a month's furlough. During this time, I want each and every one of you to take care of what you need to. Tomorrow we will start the crew exchange to prep the ship for Mars and the upgrade. You all need to talk to your families, make sure they understand what happened to you and why. Contact GASA or myself if you need anything at all. Once we are back onboard, we will proceed to Mars, spend about 3 weeks there and we receive orders. Now enjoy the food and relax."

Chapter 4

REVELATION

August 1, 2169 0800 Hours

It's hard to believe that two months ago, I was a healthy, 37-year-old male, a doctor in the thick of his career. I've been a woman a little over a month and it's as normal as if I had been female all my life. We are back on Earth, preparing to tell our families about what has happened to us. I sent my parents a few messages to prepare them. They know that something's happened to me and that my appearance has changed. I am so nervous. I've always had a good relationship with them but this is a serious test. I traveled to Baltimore to meet them since that was the closest Earth-Space port to them. They lived in Aberdeen, Maryland about 45 minutes' drive time from the city. The Inner Harbor was one of our favorite places to go. We met at the Argosy Café just up from the wharf. I dressed as gender neutral as I could, but I couldn't fight the need for minimal makeup. Not glam but to just look presentable. I put a reserved sign on the table next to mine in order for them to be able to come in and sit down. I figured they would be able to brace themselves easier that way. I saw them come and the host brought them to their table as I requested. I gave them a few minutes and they chatted nervously. "What do you think Darius looks like now?" My Mom was always curious about things. She read anything and everything she found about health, quality of life and the like. My dad was a retired Army colonel. "I couldn't imagine. Who knows what he was exposed to on Venus. When I was a kid, getting to Mars was a big deal. Now you can vacation there and be back for work in a matter of hours. God only knows what he saw on that planet, or what saw him."
I couldn't prolong the event much more. I stood up and went to their

table. "Mr. and Mrs. Obama?"

"Yes?" My Mom smiled a polite smile but was still worried about her son. I tried not to tear up. My Mom looked into my eyes as only a mother could and her smile turned into shock. "Darius? Is that you?"

"Yes, Mom. It's me. This is what I needed to tell you."

Both my parents went pale. Mom spoke first. "Wha…what happened?"

"I will explain, but first please look at this." I handed her a medi-pad with my original chip in it. Being a former nurse, she knew how to read the data and knew how to administer a quick DNA scan. I held out my hand and she scanned it. This confirmed I was her child, though no longer her son. My Dad spoke first. "Dorothy? Is it him?"

"Yes, Philip. It is."

"Dear Lord, what happened?"

I sat down next to my father. "When we went to Venus, we found amazing alien technology. All types of data, research that will change the world, for the better mostly."

"Incredible." My Dad was stunned.

"When we on Venus, we discovered an alien structure, well not so alien, and we found a machine. A device that held the sum knowledge of the inhabitants of that world."

"What do you mean, 'not so alien'?"

"The structure was a Greek temple. Other structures were Roman."

"Are you saying that the Greek and Roman gods were from Venus?"

"Yes. They were real people. But much like their mythology, pride and lust for power was their downfall."

My father stood up. "I need to use the bathroom." He walked off and I was a little shocked. My mother sat for a moment. "Don't worry, Dear he just needs some time to process all of this."

"Thanks, Mom."

"Sweetie, I don't mean to be rude, but, is this something you wanted?"

"No, Mom. This was a complete and total accident. The real tragedy is that had we found the data earlier, we could have reversed it. We were women too long for the antidote to work on us."

"I see." She seemed to brighten a little. "Can I ask- "

"Mom, you can ask me anything."

"Are you complete? I mean are you fully female?"

"Yes, we were altered at the molecular level so the cells, glands, blood chemistry, everything was changed. It was as if I was born this way."

"Amazing." Her nurse's curiosity started to come out. "So you have a vagina?"

"Not only that, I have a fully operational reproductive system."

"So I can have grandchildren-" she stopped mid-sentence and became sad. "Do you still like girls? I mean are you gay?"

"No. Another effect of the serum is that I prefer men now-and before you ask, when I was male I did like women. It was like a gradual switch being flipped." Dad came back and sat down. "So, what now?"

"Well, after this furlough, I will return to the Kennedy and go to Mars, then we are heading out farther into the solar system and then, deep space."

"What about your condition?"

"I can't change it. We can prevent it, now even change other people back provided they haven't been a woman too long."

"What does that mean?" My Dad seemed a little upset but kept his cool. I actually think he was trying to understand. "It means that someone who had been exposed to the serum, can be cured as long as they are treated within 3 weeks of exposure. After 4 weeks, a chromosomal lock closes and the affected person is stuck as a female."

"Didn't you have females on your ship? How did it affect them?"

"We researched that. They were not affected."

"So you can't change back?"

"No, Dad. I'm sorry."

"You have nothing to be sorry about. You did nothing wrong."

"Thanks, Dad."

"Well, Darius isn't a girl's name. Are you going to change it?"

"I was thinking of Daria. I didn't think about changing my name until we found out that the change was permanent. It takes some getting used to."

Dad seemed to relax. "I'll bet. Well I know this must have been hard for you. Have you told your brother?"

"No. Not sure when I will see him."

"You have 30 days right? We will find some time for a family dinner."

"Sounds great. Speaking of dinner-"
"Yes! I'm starving after all this emoting. Let's order."

Chapter 5

FURLOUGH

August 10, 2169 1330 Hours

It was a beautiful, midsummer day on Nantucket. I was in a sundress and drinking a Martian Foom. We have had property here for a few generations, ever since my great-great grandfather was President of the United States. Grampy B (as we called Barack Obama) loved coming here. According to my Dad, he said it was peaceful yet elegant. Grampy B was instrumental in getting same sex and transgender issues passed. Unfortunately, he knew nothing of national and global economics so he was viewed as a mediocre president. My father respected him but didn't agree with much of his politics. He was a conservative but not one to always tow the party line. He may not agree with same sex relations but he did want to see them hurt either. I was always a centrist, but my father and I usually saw eye to eye most of the time.
The wind was pleasant as it blew across the patio and through my dress. I was sunbathing a little and I saw someone on the beach. He was tall and rugged and had a dog. He looked familiar but he wasn't close enough to recognize. He had bronze skin and a sharp haircut. I couldn't seem to stop staring at him as my Mom came out to the patio. "You remember him?"
"He looks familiar but I can't place him."
"It's been awhile. That's Bill Wallace."
"That's Billy Wallace? The kid I played with every summer here?"
"Sure is. Turned into a handsome man, didn't he?"
"I'll say!" I was surprised at my extremely feminine reaction. It even

surprised me.

"Well, you're all girl now. Want to meet him?"

"Gee, I'm not sure. I ship out September 1."

"You don't need to marry him, dear. Just talk to him."

"I just might."

"How about I invite him to the mixer tonight? It'll be just a few friends."

"Oh Mom, I not sure I'm ready for a social event."

"You don't need to tell them anything."

"Right, but what will you tell people? All of a sudden you have a brand new thirty-seven year old daughter?"

"We'll tell them you are our niece from Somerville."

"Only if anyone asks."

"All right, Sweetie."

"Thanks, Mom."

I didn't know what was going to happen that night but one thing was for sure; I was never going to tell anyone that Dr. Darius Obama is now Daria Obama. It seemed too overwhelming to try and explain the whole process to casual acquaintances and old friends. I decided to keep a low profile at the mixer. I got up and walked off the patio onto the beach. I wasn't trying to get Bill's attention, but somehow, I wanted it. As I walked in the opposite direction of him, I realized quite plainly that I was attracted to him. I was never one to wear my heart on my sleeve, but something in my newly female soul woke up and I felt warm. I kept walking and decided to take my dress off. I was wearing a modest but flattering bikini underneath. No one was around so I felt comfortable doing that. There was an outcropping about 100 yards from the house and it was private. I liked to go over there to read or just think. There was a natural tide pool there and the water is always relatively warm. I found a rock to sit on and pondered how I was going to deal with the people at this party. I decide to take my top off and bathe a little in the pool. I liked the way the water felt on my skin. It was soothing. I closed my eyes and untied my top. I let it float in the water and cleared my mind. It seemed like an hour had passed. "Hello!" I jumped a mile and grabbed my top. "Who are you?"

"Bill. Bill Wallace. Sorry I scared you. I will stay over here until you compose yourself." I put my top back on quickly and got up. I started walking back to the house and Bill followed. "Are you ok?"

"Yes. I'm fine."

"I didn't know you were there. I've been coming to this cove since I was I kid."

"Me too." I just wanted to get into the house.

"Really? How come I've never seen you?"

"You have!" I caught myself. "I mean I used to come with my cousin."

"Who's your cousin?"

"Darius Obama."

"Ol' Danger Man! We used to hang out every summer! How is he?"

"Fine! He's fine. Goodbye." I dashed up onto the patio and hurried into the house. I was scared and a little embarrassed. I was also aroused. I think I was thrown off because I found Bill attractive and I didn't want to. The last thing I needed right now was a relationship and as a newly minted female I hadn't quite figured out my emotions. I couldn't help thinking about him as I rushed for the safety of the beach house.

August 10, 2169 1800 Hours

"Party Time, Chumps!" It was a favorite joke of my father's. He loved old Youtube videos and he would quote one every now and then. Usually, he was the only one who got it. The party was larger than I expected, larger than I would have liked. Still, I had gotten over the earlier embarrassment and decided to enjoy the party. I saw many old family friends and acquaintances, none of who recognized me. I was made up to the hilt, mostly because I'd come to enjoy it but also to disguise myself as much as possible. I didn't know how many people there knew about the Venus Mission or its effects to the Kennedy crew but the last thing I wanted was attention. I thought the name Daria might be too obvious so earlier I researched some family names and decided on something different. The family had a lot of roots in Africa so an African name seemed appropriate.

I came down in a white maxi-skirt with black and white pumps. I had a silver, shimmery blouse that edged my shoulders and a wide black belt with a buckle. I kept my hair down and locked in place with an ionic headband. "You look lovely, Dear!" My mother was so proud. She brought me into the great room and starts introducing me to some old friends as her niece from Somerville. I was glad I was able to educate Mom and Dad about this new persona. "Marla, this is Endana, my niece."

"It's nice to meet you, Endana." This woman had given me piano lessons for years. "You look so much like Darius! You two could be twins."

"He's a few years older than me." I looked and felt barely thirty years old so I played it that way. The next few hours were pleasant. People were accepting me as Endana and that suited me just fine. I had just finished a decent size dinner and I was sipping a cognac when I felt a cold chill. "You clean up nicely." The playfully sarcastic tone belonged to Bill Wallace. I spun around and saw him standing there, dressed too well for a small gathering. "I'd hope I would see you here."

"Well then, there you go."

"You never told me your name."

"Nope, I didn't." I was more prepared to deal with him now.

"Sorry again about scaring you earlier."

"No problem. Endana Obama."

"Bill Wallace."

"I remember."

"Care to retire to the patio?"

"Okay." I felt less threatened by my emotions now that I had another identity to hide behind. I figured it would be nice to catch up with Bill as much as possible under the circumstances. We brought our drinks out to the patio and sat down. "Beautiful evening." Bill was obviously working his charm.

"Yes it is."

"So what do you do?"

"I'm a doctor for GASA. I'm home on furlough until the end of the month."

"Wow. So you're headed into space!"

"That's right."

"What ship are you on?"

"The Nunya."

"The Nunya?"

"Yes, the Nunya business because it's classified."

We both laughed and Bill said, "I understand. Have you had any interesting missions?"

"Yes, but again, nunya. There are still people that question the morality of us going into space."

"You're kidding. We've been in space for over a hundred years!"

"I know but ever since faster than light travel became possible, and the Mars colonization, it's became an issue. The anti-space crowd is afraid we're going to spread imperialism and our rigid morals across the galaxy."

"You disagree?"

"Of course. The fact we can now travel throughout and even outside our own solar system changes the whole question of existence. Who or what is out there is the ultimate question to be answered. I find it fascinating."

"You're brilliant."

"I'm tired. What time is it?"

"It's about 10:30."

"Hmm I didn't do much today. I guess I'm used to being busy."

"Well, I'd like to continue our conversation, say maybe over lunch tomorrow?"

For some reason that caught me off guard. I've never been asked out by a man and since now I am fully female, I rather liked the idea.

"Sure. That'd be okay."

"Great! I'll pick you up at noon."

"Okay."

My first date. With my old childhood summer friend. I couldn't believe it. My female mind was beginning to think about what to wear and how I would enter the room. I was excited, and a little scared. I bounced back into the great room and most of the guests had left or were heading out. My mother was picking up and I couldn't contain myself. "Mom! You won't believe it! I got a date!"

My Mom's face went white, then red with joy. She smiled and said, "That's great Sweetie! With who?"

"Bill Wallace."

"That's amazing." She pulled me into the alcove. "Does he know?"

"Know what? Oh- "I realized what she meant almost immediately. "No, he has no idea."

"Is that what you want?"

"Well for now. I can't really have a relationship, anyway. I have to report back to duty in 3 weeks."

"Sweetie, just be careful. A woman's heart is a powerful thing."
"I'll be careful, Mom. Besides he's just an old friend. We'll just get caught up."
"Okay, Honey."
I wasn't tired yet and since it would take a tremendous amount of alcohol to get me drunk, I decided to walk on the beach. I looked out into the evening sea. I thought about space and then I thought of Bill and what kind of future we'd have. The problem was I knew how to be a doctor, but I wasn't sure if I knew how to be a woman. The virus was complete in that I developed a female reproductive system so I guess that the only male part of me left was in my head. I decided I would enjoy my time with Bill but not romantically. I was hoping I could pull that off.

Chapter 6

FIRST DATE

August 2, 2169 0730 Hours

I woke up about 7:30am, and decided to take a swim in the pool. The ocean was pretty cool in the morning so I deferred to the warmer water. Once I finished and walked into the kitchen, Mom had a fresh pot of coffee brewed. She was old fashioned in many ways and coffee was one of those treats. That's the great thing about Nantucket, it was a slower pace and a lot of old fashioned customs were kept alive. After breakfast, I used the com to see how the ship's progress was coming. The work was ahead of schedule and Tanner put out a directive that furlough would not be cut short if the work was finished ahead of schedule. So I had another three weeks to relax and enjoy the late summer. I watched a movie and went upstairs to get ready for my lunch date. I again went through several outfits and finally decided on a casual summer dress and leggings. I added a wide hat and low heeled shoes and a little jewelry to cap off the outfit. I came downstairs and my Dad had just come in from fishing. "Hey Kiddo. You look great."
"Thanks Dad. I have a lunch date."
"Oh really? With who?"
"Bill Wallace."
"Really? Hmm. Are you okay with that?"
"Yeah. I talked to Mom about it last night."
"All right. Well, have fun." I heard a bit of concern in his voice.
"It'll be fine, Dad. We're just going as friends."
"Oh so you told him?"

"No. And I won't unless I have to."

"Just be careful, Sweetie. You have to go into space in a few weeks. It wouldn't be fair to start a relationship now."

"I know, Dad. Just friends. Promise."

"Okay, Sweetie. See you later."

My Dad never called me Sweetie. He's gotten used to having a daughter so I have no complaints.

August 2, 2169 Noon

Bill showed up, noon on the dot. He had a hoverbike and I had never ridden one before. "Howdy! Ready for lunch?"

"Sure but on this?"

"You can ride side saddle."

"That's okay." I hopped up and straddled the bike like an old pro.

"You sure you've never been on one of these?"

"I'm a quick study. Let's go."

We whooshed around and rode to downtown. Bill pointed to the Handlebar Café and I nodded. We landed the bike in the parking lot where Candle St meets Washington. He powered down the bike and took the fusion key. "Here we are. Hope you're hungry."

"Well, I could eat." Another benefit to the Eleusian virus is the ability to eat whatever I wanted and not gain weight. Not even water weight. We went into the quaint shop and sat down. We ordered sandwiches and then dessert.

"Wow, you are a healthy girl. That's good."

"Why is that 'good'?" I probably sounded more annoyed than I actually was. "It shows security. You're very confident in yourself."

"You have to be to survive space, and medical school."

Bill laughed. I smiled. He has dimples. I never noticed that before. It was endearing. "How is your cousin, Darius? I haven't seen him in years."

"He's also a doctor. He's at the Mars colony." I was hoping a little white lie would shift his focus. "How about you? What are you doing these days?"

"I'm a lawyer."

"Really? For who?"

"The Anti-Space Initiative."

I nearly choked on my scone. "The WHAT?"

"Relax, I just do legal research for them."

"Why would you work for them? They almost shut down the space program!"

"I work for them so there is someone pro-space who is keeping them balanced. Plus, I had a friend who was badly injured during the construction of one of the launch platforms. I just wanted the workers to be safe and protected."

"I see. I'm sorry about your friend."

"Thanks. Anyway, I think going to space is great. I just don't want anyone to die."

"That's the risk we all take. You can't venture into the unknown without taking risks. Sometimes it's the ultimate price. We all hope not to have to pay it, but we all know it's a possibility."

Bill nodded. "I understand. I guess I want to explore the cosmos from the safety of my living room."

I had to smile at that. "Where is your office?"

"Boston. During the nice weather I like to take the bike. I can be in the city within an hour at 105 mph."

"That's pretty fast." I was beginning to feel that warm sensation again. I figured a ride into the city might take my mind off of it. "Let's go. Show me your office."

"Really? It's just a boring law office."

"Actually, I want to go really fast on your bike." I heard the words come out of my mouth like a sensuous vixen looking for more than a ride.

"Okay!" He seemed as excited as I was and we were off. He paid the bill in cash and we were off like a shot. He fired up the fusion drive and we took off fast. He followed the coast to the city and circled the downtown area. He had a spot on State Street but he parked it on the roof. Roof parking was for executives and emergencies but everyone was on vacation so we had the place to ourselves.

"That was the fastest I've ever gone!" I was going to get a hoverbike after my turn in space.

"That *was* fun!" Bill was flushed. He pressed his hand to the entry plate and it slid open. We walked into a large vestibule. The windows of the vestibule protected the inner office from the high winds.

"This is my office. I have four people who work for me so I just do a lot of coordinating and fact checking." He placed his hand on another entry plate and the doors slid open. We walked fast to his office and he opened it up. "Care for a drink?" He walked slower towards the bar. I went up behind him and found that I could not control myself any longer. He turned around and I was right behind him. I grabbed him and started kissing him. He reciprocated and we fell down onto the wide couch and made out for half an hour. Fortunately, I came to my senses and pulled away. "That was nice."

"That was awesome."

"I just don't want to lead you on. I'm going into space in a few weeks. I'm committed."

"I know. But, I like you, very much."

"We will take it one day at a time."

"Okay." I kissed him again. I never thought I would enjoy it this much. I just hope I can keep it together for the next three weeks.

"Say how about we go to Maine for lobster?"

"Absolutely!"

About another hour later we were in York Beach. I loved York, because it was the first family vacation I could remember. We walked the beach and when we found a secluded area the smooching would continue. I was enjoying being a woman, maybe for the first time but I really wanted to keep things simple.

We enjoyed exploring old haunts and new areas and finally we found a place that served excellent lobster. Bill was a perfect gentleman and I appreciated that. I hoped I could remain a lady and not want more. For most of the day, since the office make out session, I wanted more. I was afraid that by the end of the day, my urges may be more than I could bear.

We were walking by a convenience mart and I excused myself. "I need some things. I'm just going to stop in here for a minute."

"Okay." Bill was a dutiful date. I slipped into the old fashioned store and bought some gum, lip balm and, reluctantly, some birth control material. I wasn't sure how my new physiology would take intimacy, so prepared for both of us. I didn't want to lead Bill on, so I paid for the items stuffed them as deep into my purse as I could. "It will be dark soon. The bike has no lights so we should head back to Nantucket."

"Okay. Sounds good."

We got on the bike and the shimmy of the fusion drive loosened my teeth. As the bike rose, I realized I had pretty sensuous feelings for

Bill and I felt I may seal the deal when we get back. I'm glad I went to the store. We flew about 12 feet above the water but kept close the coast line. We got down around the coast of Salem, Mass and he landed. "What's wrong?"

"Seems like the fusion drive is bogging down. I just need to take a quick look."

"Okay." I welcomed the break though it wasn't a long trip, also, Bill didn't seem the mechanic type but I took his word for it. "We'll need to let the beryllium core recharge. It should take about half an hour. We can look around a bit." I've only been to Salem a few times. They've been able to preserve a lot of the history of the town from what I understand.

"There's a biergarten over here. Care for a brew?"

"Sure, but will we have enough light to get back?"

"Yeah, we won't be long."

He seemed relaxed about the idea so I agreed. We walked down from the wharf and found the place. "This is one of the oldest places in town-still operating that is."

"Interesting. How do you know so much about this place?"

"Went to college here. I like to come back from time to time."

We went into the bar and they had hundreds of brews. Many on tap. We enjoyed a few and it got dark. I think Bill was trying to get me tipsy. I noticed he was fairly tight so I played along. "Bill, it's dark now! How are we going to see to get home?" I added some drunken giggling.

"I don't think we are, at least tonight anyway. We should get rooms."

"Where do you suggest?"

"The New Hawthorne Hotel. Nice amenities and I am a member."

"Okay but no hoverbike riding. We are too drunk." I wanted to say it out loud so he knew that I knew that weren't going anywhere tonight."

We stumbled two blocks back towards the wharf (which worked out because it was half way back to the charging station) and found the hotel. We went to the desk and the hotel clerk gave us two keys. Bill insisted that I have my own room. We found them and spilled into the first one. Bill was feeling no pain. He excused himself and went to the bathroom. I took the precaution of lifting my skirt and putting a contraceptive patch on my inner thigh. I had committed to the idea that we were going to be intimate tonight so my prior planning was well timed. Bill had been in the bathroom for some time so I paused my drunk act and checked on him. "Bill? Bill, are you okay?" I knocked on the door and no response. I immediately opened the door and there was Bill, passed out on the floor. "My hero," I thought. I checked his vitals and he was fine, except for being exceptionally drunk. I figured he wouldn't notice my enhanced strength so I picked him up like a rag doll and put him to bed. A thought occurred to me. Was he trying to get me drunk? I pretty much matched him drink for drink. He didn't know that it was impossible for me to get drunk. I've kept secret many of the 'improvements' since the change. I hope the rest of the Kennedy crew did the same. The irony is that I was ready to sleep with him and would have without much convincing.

Chapter 7

FIRST DATE, SECOND DAY

August 3, 2169 0209 Hours

I removed the patch from my thigh and laid down next to Bill. I decided to stay with him to make sure he'd be all right. He might even think we had made the move. I didn't really need much sleep anymore but I like to keep the routine and I did feel better afterwards. Another effect was that I could sleep as deep or as light as I wanted to. I laid back on the bed and I thought about having a life as a civilian. A husband, kids, and a comfortable career as a local doctor. Sounded nice. Yet, the stars called to me. I didn't think I'd spent my entire career with GASA, exploring space, although I wanted to see what was out there. To be one of the first to contact an alien race. I had dreams like that since I was a kid. I looked at Bill and wondered if he would wait for me. Would that be fair to him? Would I survive to come back? These were all the reasons I stayed single-to go into space unfettered. I slept for a few hours and got up. Bill was still passed out so I went down to the restaurant for coffee and a light breakfast. I decided to let Bill sleep it off and went exploring in downtown Salem. I was charmed by its old world flavor. The old colonial buildings, the House of the Seven Gables and the wharf. I stopped into a little book shop called The Omega House and looked over some New Age books. The New Age movement was a popular fad about 100 years ago and this store catered to those who still gave it any credibility. I found something interesting, though. There was a section of books in the corner that looked like no one paid attention to it for a long time. There were ancient texts, like *'Chariots of the*

Gods?', and *'Out On A Limb'*, but there was one that was very unassuming. It spoke of ancient beings and their thirst for conquest. *'Gods and Man, Are we Truly Alone in the Cosmos?'* It piqued my interest so I purchased it and went back to the hotel.

I went to the room and Bill was in the shower. I decided to put the patch on again, just to be safe. I started to have thoughts about him naked in the shower. I hadn't showered for a while, so while I had the urge to hop in the shower with him, I still wasn't sure of his intentions. I knocked on the door and cracked it open. "Bill? You okay?"

"I'll live," He moaned.

"You really tied one on last night."

"Yeah, I know. I'm sorry. I hope I didn't ruin your evening."

"No, it was fine. I guess I didn't drink as much as I thought."

"Really? I thought you matched me dead on."

"Well I never finish a drink. The waiter wasn't happy with me."

"Oh."

"It's 10am. I think you can still get breakfast downstairs."

"No, just coffee. It's about all I can handle."

"All right."

Bill didn't seem in the mood for anything other than recovering so I went along. I brought up some coffee and we went to the veranda. There was a love seat and we sat closely. Bill still had a hint of alcohol odor but was functional. "Well. We do we have planned for today?"

"It's been a nice weekend. I'm not obligated to anything today."

"Awesome. The hoverbike should be fully charged by now. We can cruise around town or head back Nantucket, or go back to the city."

I moved in close to his face. "I'd prefer to stay put for a little while." I took control and kissed him. We made out for about an hour and I couldn't take it anymore. "Let's go." He obediently followed me with his hand in mine and we rushed back to the room. The patch would only be good for another day so I didn't waste it. I was a virgin, in the female sense, so many of these sensations and emotions I was feeling for the first time. I wanted to wait until I was married but I just couldn't help myself. The lovemaking process seemed different than I thought. My cells seemed to vibrate and I felt like I was charged with electricity. About 2 hours later, we lay in bed, tired but relaxed. "That was amazing." Bill said.

"Thanks. You were pretty good yourself."
"Just pretty good?"
"Well, it takes practice."

August 3, 2169 1145 Hours

We decided to check out Salem State University before we headed back to Nantucket. We found the campus and enjoyed its academic splendor. Bill showed me his old dorm, we toured the campus with some prospective students and got some food at the O'Keefe Center. We went up to the Sky Campus (a floating platform that housed the astronomy department and a planetarium) to visit the astronomy department and see a show at the planetarium. Unfortunately, the pleasant atmosphere was interrupted by some Anti-Space protesters. A group had formed on the landing platform with their tablets and mesh digital picket signs.
"Keep Man on the Ground!"
"Stay on your own planet!"
"Don't pollute the universe!"
College campuses have always been hotbeds of liberalism and protesting. Young students learn about many issues and then find time to oppose them. Their idealism was admirable, albeit sometimes misplaced. Bill and I decided to go back down to the ground and avoid the commotion. The protesters blocked us from the launch point so we tried to work our way over. I noticed a young boy, a freshman I would imagine, who seemed lost and nervous. The crowd was starting to get unruly and Bill and I were separated. The safety field had been turned off and the controls smashed. I was able to force my way through but I needed to find that boy. I could see the hoverbike and Bill had left the fusion key in it. The nervous young man was dangerously close to the edge and it was a half mile drop to the ground. I tried to keep an eye on him as he was being pushed to the edge. I had a bad feeling about his immediate future so I fought to get toward the bike. Finally, I leaped over 3 people and landed on the bike. I fired it up just in time to see the young man slip off the edge to certain death. Instinctively, I gunned the hoverbike and dove after him. I knew how to build speed and I raced the bike directly toward the falling student. I was on him in a couple of seconds and grabbed

his arm. The angle he was at allowed me to use momentum to swing him up and behind me. He grabbed me around the waist and held on for dear life as I pulled up on the controls. The bike shifted upwards and I gunned the engine to stop our descent. We bumped the ground but shot up again. I did a full circle around to blow off the momentum. Once we landed I asked him, "Are you okay?" He nodded then vomited off to the side. "Are you sure? I am a doctor." He composed himself enough to say, "Yes. Thank you! You saved my life."

"Well, like I said, I'm doctor. That's what I do. What's your name?" Jake. Jake Stevens."

"Go home and rest, Jake. You've had a traumatic day."

"I will. Thanks, Doc."

He wobbled off toward some buildings and I took a moment. I realized I forgot something up at Sky Campus. "Bill!" I fired up the fusion drive and climbed into the sky. I took my time so I looked out over the city as I went upward. I landed at the platform and Bill was waiting for me. I smiled the sweetest smile I could muster and landed. "Hi, Bill."

"Are you okay? I was scared to death!"

"Yes, I'm fine."

"Did you save him?"

"Yes. Jake is fine. Shaken, but nothing a hot shower and a good night's sleep won't cure."

"That was incredible! How did you do it?"

"I couldn't have done it without you. I watched you ride the bike and I am a quick study. As a GASA doctor, you have to be creative under pressure."

"You are amazing." Bill planted a passionate kiss on my lips.

"Let's go home." I was ready for a quiet evening.

August 3, 2169 1800 Hours

We took our time flying back to Nantucket. I wanted to see my parents and sleep in my own bed. I felt a little more tired than usual. Bill landed the bike in front of my house and we sat on the front porch. We didn't talk much but we did want to see each other again. I thought that a full day apart would give us time to recharge. Bill had some business to take care of anyway so we made a dinner date on Tuesday. I kissed him for as long as I could stand it and we said goodbye. "So Tuesday, then? About 4pm?" He really didn't want to leave but being ever the gentleman, he gave me some space.

"Count on it." I giggled.

We parted ways and I floated into the house. My Dad was watching television. "Hi, Dad."

"Hi Sweetie. How was your date?"

"It was amazing."

"I'll bet. Have you seen the news?"

"No."

My father had that sarcastic, joking tone in his voice. "Apparently, some lady doctor in Salem saved a young student from certain death. The young man was the Governor's son."

He handed me a tablet. "You're kidding."

"Nope. They didn't get her name though."

"Wow. That's a good thing."

"This is why I didn't have any problem about your change. You are still the same caring, amazing person that I raised. Plus it wasn't your fault."

"What wasn't my fault?"

"Your gender change."

"What if it was?"

"What do you mean?"

"Let's say that I wanted to change into a woman. Would you feel the same way you do now?"

"I honestly don't know, Sweetie. It's unprecedented. But what I do know is this: if even if you did, I would never stop loving you. No matter what. I would whatever I had to protect you, too. But see, I knew I raised you right. Whatever happened I knew you were a person of great integrity. So I wasn't worried."

"Thanks, Dad."

"You bet. Love you."

"Love you, too. Where's Mom?"

"On her way back from her Alzheimer's treatment. She only has a few more."

"Great. I'm sure that's a big relief."

"You betcha. So how are you going to handle this hero thing?"

"Handle it?"

"People are going to want to know more about you. 'The woman doctor that saved the governor's son'. People will be curious."

"Crap. That's not what I wanted."

"You may need to keep a low profile then. You can camp out here til it blows over."

"I may need to cancel my date."

"With Bill? When?"

"Tomorrow at 4pm. We were going to grab an early dinner. Maybe a movie."

"If you stay local, it may be easier. I suggest staying here on the island. Oran Mor Restaurant may be open or the American Season."

"That's a good idea. Let me give Bill a call." I got my tablet and dialed. "Hey there. I was hoping you'd call."

"Yeah. I gazed at him for a moment. "Anyway, about tomorrow."

"Are we still on?"

"Yes! Of course. But I was hoping we could stay on the island."

"Shunning the spotlight, are we?"

"You've heard."

"Yes and I am proud of you-and still very amazed."

"Thanks." I mooned over him more. "What do you say to Oran Mor or American Season?"

"The Season has live entertainment."

"The Season it is. See you at 4."

"See you then." We both hesitated to hang up. Finally, I snapped out of my school girl fog and said goodbye.

Dad spoke up with concern, "Not to be a downer, but what happens when you ship out? You're not supposed to have any ties here."

"I know, and he knows I'm going back into space."

"I just don't want you to get sidetracked. Just be careful."

"Okay, Dad,"

Chapter 8

PERFECT NIGHTS, UNWANTED ATTENTION

August 4, 2169 Noontime

I finished a swim in the pool. August is a funny month in New England. It can be hot one minute and cool the next. I wanted to be fresh for my date. I put on a robe and sat on the patio. I put on the news to see if there was any more coverage of my heroic event. It was more prevalent than I hoped. Fortunately, they didn't have my name and I only volunteered it a few times at the party. Hopefully, this will blow over fast.

"An anonymous heroine saves the governor's son. Coming Up." I really didn't want to watch but I figured I'd better. "During an Anti-Space protest, a malfunctioning safety barrier allowed a Salem State student to fall off the college's famed Sky Campus. A woman hops over some of the protestors to save Jake Stevens, only son of Governor Stevens, when he accidentally slips off the platform. The governor had this to say:

'I am extremely grateful for the life of my son. He's the only family I have since my wife died and I would be lost without him. To the brave lady who saved his life, you have my eternal thanks.'

We will continue to cover this story as it develops."

What else can 'develop'? I was hoping they wouldn't try to find me. I went in and had a light snack so I wouldn't ruin my appetite for my early dinner with Bill. I got another call. It was Captain Tanner.

"Hey Doc," she giggled. "How's your vacation?"

"Pretty good, Commander. Yours?"

"I've actually been having a lot of fun. I saw the story."

"I figured."

"What are you going to do?" She got serious for a moment.

"Nothing, for now. Hopefully it will blow over."

"Well, if you need a place to lay low, let me know. As a member of the Senior Staff, you have the authority to return to the Kennedy anytime you want."

"Ok, thanks. I should be fine. Although I will probably go back a few days early to make sure sickbay and the medical labs are ready."

"Sounds good. Keep me posted on your situation, please. Also we should get together for drinks before too long."

"I'd like that."

"See you."

The view screen went dark. I decided I would read for a while. Dad was sentimental about some things and he always kept paper books around. He said he likes the feel and the fact that he doesn't have to charge it like a tablet. I liked those things, too. I decided to read a classic and chose, 'A Tale of Two Cities'. I stayed in my robe but took off my bathing suit. I went back out to the patio and relaxed. I fell asleep reading and had the oddest dream. I was on a spaceship. It was unfamiliar but I knew where things were. A muscular, amazingly attractive man was standing by the long window, looking out into the cosmos. I could see the stars but I did not recognize them. He turned to me and motioned for me to come. I was curious but I don't think I could have refused him. He began to kiss my neck. A feeling of love and passion came over me and I succumbed to his passion. He picked me up and brought me into a chamber with a large dais that I took for a bed. He made love to me and then I woke up. I was warm and flushed. It was so real! I looked at the time and it was 3:45pm. "Damn! I'm going to be late!" I thought. I decided to go casual and grabbed a pair of jeans and a comfortable top. The top was soft but it had a very low neckline. I didn't think about that and threw on some simple make up. I ran a brush through my hair and put it into a ponytail. Somehow, I got it together and got to the door. Bill was walking up to the door as I dashed out, almost crashing into him. He caught me. "Hi!"

"Hey there. Sorry I thought I was going to be late."

"I figured I'd come down and escort you."

"Always the gentleman. Thanks."

We walked down to North Centre Street. Fortunately, no one seemed to recognize me so I relaxed and planned to have a pleasant evening.

"Hey just to be clear, please don't tell anyone about the rescue. I only have a few days of furlough left and I'd like to enjoy it in peace."

"Sure, no problem." Bill seemed a little bummed out about that comment. He shook it off and we proceeded to the restaurant. We sat down at a nice table and ordered drinks. Bill seemed a little sad but tried to stay upbeat. "You said you only had a few more days. I thought your furlough was till the end of the month."

"Well I wanted to go back a few day early to get up to speed on my new sick bay and medical labs. We are heading to Mars and beyond so I wanted to make sure everything was ready."

"Ah. That makes sense."

"You seem down."

"I guess I didn't want things to end."

"They're not over yet."

"I know."

"Bill, in the short time we've known each other, I have grown quite fond of you but you knew from the beginning that I wasn't staying around long."

"I guess I didn't want it to end." He took my hand. "Any chance you could stay around for me?"

I was a little angry at the comment, but I understood how he felt. "I was honest with you from the start. To be honest, I am very fond of you, too. If things could be different, maybe there could be an 'us'. I guess we're not too old for summer romances."

"I'm sorry to do that to you. Let's enjoy the time we have." Bill came to accept the situation, though just barely. If didn't want to go back into space so badly, I would stay. But who knows what the future holds?

We enjoyed the rest of the evening without any melancholic moods. We laughed and walked on a different beach. We made out. Fortunately, I remembered to use a new birth control patch and glad that I did. We made out on the beach and enjoyed each other completely. It turned into a perfect night.

August 5, 2169 0812 Hours

It was the first time I saw Bill's bungalow. It was elegant yet modest.
I woke up to the smell of a homemade breakfast including bacon and
coffee. I found a robe and walked out to the kitchen. "Smells great."
I kissed him on the lips. He was shirtless and well cut. He took the
eggs off the burner and put them on the warmer. The bacon was
almost done. "Hope you're hungry. Breakfast is the only thing I
know how to make."
"I'm famished, and not just for breakfast!", I giggled. I kissed Bill
again. I was energized and happy, and now so was Bill. We were
going to spend the day together so I put on a tank top over my bikini
top and a mini-skirt over bikini underwear. We cuddled on the couch
and napped a bit. About 11:00 there was a knock on the door. It was
my father. "Morning, Sweetie, Bill. I have some troubling news."
"What is it, Dad?"
"Someone identified you at the restaurant last night. They contacted
the island press." I got a tablet and brought up the newswire. The
headline read, "Local Island Resident-Heroic Doctor?"
"So they're not sure?"
"I guess. That's a little too close to home, though."
"I hate the press."
"I know, Sweetheart. It's a double-edged sword sometimes."
"Well, I'm really going to have to keep a low profile now."
"Only your mother and I know you're here."
"You could stay here for the rest of the week. Private access to the
beach and, well me." Bill was liking the idea of us shacking up for a
week. "I guess I can hang out here."
Dad sighed. "I will get your things. See you in a little while,
Sweetie." I think my father liked having a daughter he could protect
and dote on. "So, Roomie, what now?"
Bill didn't say anything but swooped in and kissed me. We made out
again.

August 8, 2169 0900

The past few days were uneventful. Bill and I felt like we knew each other for years, and I guess in a way, we have. I don't know if I would ever tell him I was once Darius Obama. Truth be told, I never thought about my male life. My parents had accepted me as their daughter (niece for the rest of the world) and Bill was happy. But then, those thoughts came back. Would I be happy in space without Bill? Was I ready for the civilian life? Did I want it? My desire for exploration had not diminished but I wondered if it was still my top priority. At the same time, I remembered the pact I made with myself, shortly after my gender change. Keep going, into space, because if I didn't, if I gave it up before getting out there, would I regret it? So space it was. Maybe for not as long as I thought if Bill was going to wait. I was up playing a game when there was a knock on the door. I froze for a moment then checked the security pad. There were two state troopers standing outside with an envelope. I decided to handle it myself. I answered the door. "Dr. Obama?"

"What can I do for you gentlemen?"

"On behalf of the Governor, he'd like you to have this." He handed me an old fashioned invitation. It was from Governor Stevens, inviting me and a 'plus one' to a state banquet. It was a multi-purpose event, honoring several notable Bay Staters for various accomplishments. I asked, "Does he need an RSVP right now?"

"No. Just follow the instructions."

"All right. Thanks." The troopers departed politely and I walked back into the house. There was no way I was going to a public event. More publicity I did not need. I put the invitation down on the small table in foyer and went back to my game. Bill was up and in the bathroom. He took a shower and came out. "Was someone here?"

"Yes. The Governor found me."

"Oooh. Sorry. What'd they say?"

"He's invited me to a state dinner."

"You're not going, are you?"

"No way. Too much press."

"That's tough. It's hard to deny the governor. He doesn't like that."

"I know. Maybe I can meet him privately."

"That's a good idea. You should do that."

I got the contact information off the invite and called the main number at the State House. I spoke with the Governor's Office and they said they would clear it with the Governor himself. Bill went down to the beach and I joined him.

"How'd it go?"

"Surprisingly easy. I'm not a big fan of bureaucracy. I thought it would have been harder."

"Ah, well sometimes you hit it just right. So now what?"

"I wait. Hopefully, Stevens understands my desire for privacy and we can get this over with."

"I love you."

"Yeah, wait what?" I thought I imagined it.

Bill turned to me and looked into my eyes. "I said I love you. I did not want to say it. I didn't want it to be true. "Look, I know you are leaving, but if you had gone into space and I didn't say it to you, I would have regretted it for the rest of my life. It's your choice if you say it back, but please do not feel obligated."

I was shocked but not totally surprised. I wanted to say it because I had realized it early on. I don't wear my heart on my sleeve but with this new female persona, it was all new territory. I looked at Bill a long time and then kissed him. A rush of heat and sexual excitement buzzed through me. We laid down on the blanket and held each other. I wanted him but it seemed that us holding each other was enough for that moment. We were quiet for a long time. Finally, we stood up, and we went back to the bungalow. We were getting started when a call on the screen came in. We composed ourselves and walked over. It was the Governor, himself.

"My office says you'd like a private meeting."

"Yes sir. I have a career in GASA and I'd like to keep it unfettered."

"Very well. I understand. When is a good time?"

"I return to duty on the 27th. How about the 25th?

"We'll make it a lunch date."

"That's fine. Thank you, Governor Stevens."

August 10, 2169 0800

Bill and I had been enjoying each other for 2 days straight. I'd never done that before, even when I was in a serious relationship as a man. We were sitting down to breakfast and discussing the day. I wanted to go out and it seemed like a good day to do it. I had kept a low profile and it seems that it was effective. It was then that it occurred to me the dilemma of telling Bill the truth about my past; that I was indeed his old summertime beach buddy Darius and that I changed into a woman by an alien virus. I was still determined to go back into space. I didn't want to be tethered by a relationship, but I did truly love Bill. Like no one I'd had ever loved before. I decided to keep my secret and should I return to him, then I would tell him.

People forget space is still a very dangerous place. Exploring the unknown and all that comes with it. I was a good doctor and I wanted to make the most of my career. The durability of my new body could be tested in the outer reaches of the Solar System, and new discoveries are imminent. I've always wanted to be a part of that, but now this man has my heart and I want to give him mine. Dilemmas.

My tablet rang. It was Mom. "Morning, Sweetheart. How are you?"

"I'm fine, Mom. What's up?"

"Oh, nothing. Your Dad was saying how we haven't seen you in a while and thought you might like to come over for lunch."

"I'd like that. Is Bill invited?"

"Normally, yes but we'd like to have you to ourselves for a little while. I know you two are getting close."

"Okay. That'll be fine."

"All right sweetie. About 12:30?"

"You got it. See you then."

"Love you, Honey."

"Love you too, Mom."

I walked into the bedroom and Bill was doing some work. I took a breath. "I'm having lunch with my folks."

"Okay." Bill turned around to look at me. "Do you mind going alone? I am swamped with work. I should be able to get more of this done before dinner."

"Sure, no problem."

I didn't bother to tell him that he wasn't invited to lunch. I figured I'd leave well enough alone. I went for a swim and took a shower. I think my Mom wanted to talk to me, but I left it up to her. I got to their house right at 12:30.

"Hi Dad."

"Hi Pumpkin. Come on in."

"How are things?"

"Oh fine. Come on into the living room."

We walked into the living room and sat down. Dad seemed pensive, like he wanted to say something. "What is it, Dad?"

"Well Sweetie, I wanted to just ask, how close are you and Bill?"

"Pretty close, I guess. Why?"

"He knows you're going back into space, right?"

"Yes, Dad we talked about that."

"And you both are okay? With it?"

"Yes."

"Okay. I just needed some assurance. You two seemed to be getting along pretty well."

"I care for him. We've become close."

"Does he know? Did you tell him about the change?"

"No, I decided that since I'm going back into space, I keep that secret. Dad, you have to know that I would tell him if I were going to stay on Earth."

"Okay. You'll be up there for a year. Maybe there is a future for you two?"

"Maybe, Dad. But for now I am a GASA doctor, Chief Medical Officer for the USS Kennedy. I'd like to ride that ship for awhile."

"All right, Sweetie. I made tomato soup and grilled cheese for lunch."

"Mmm sounds great." I hugged my Dad. He is a great man and a great father. Mom came in and looked at us. She looked at Dad with a plethora of questions, I assume the same ones my Dad just asked me. He nodded and she relaxed and smiled. We enjoyed lunch and had nice afternoon. It was about three when I thought I should get back. Bill had done the majority of the cooking so tonight it was my turn. I hugged my parents and started to walk back to the bungalow. I got a call on my tablet so I found a bench on the main street and sat down. It was someone I did not recognize except for the uniform.

"Dr. Obama, I am Captain Phillip Cleveland of the GASA Judge Advocate General's office. Sorry to interrupt your furlough but we need to speak with you immediately."

"What is this about?"

"I'd rather speak to you in person."

"When?"

"First thing in the morning at 0800 hours. We can meet you on the island. You are staying with your parents still?"

"Yes." I was a little unnerved that he knew that but it was information he could have gotten from the Kennedy.

"I will meet you there. No need to dress formally."

"Okay. Thanks." I was not sure he was doing me any favors. I immediately called my parents. I told them what happened and they said it was fine to meet at their house. I walked quickly back to the bungalow to tell Bill. "What do they want with you?"

"Don't know. They are coming here so it's not something I did. At least I hope not."

"Do you want me to come with you?"

"No, another lawyer might make him nervous." Not to mention me being nervous. I figured it was something to do with what happened on Venus. I wasn't ready to tell Bill about that so I also needed time to come up with a plausible story.

I made a baked chicken catalde over pasta and a nice salad. We enjoyed some white wine and some chocolate pie. We cuddled on the couch to a movie and enjoyed the peaceful evening. I took a break and went to check my messages via the virtual com. These would be messages I get through my GASA email account. Normally, I've been getting maintenance updates and a few messages from Troy and Jamie. For some odd reason, the messages stopped yesterday morning and I seemed to be locked out. It was strange, but I figured they might be updating the servers. I shrugged it off and went back to the couch. "What's the matter?" Bill asked.

"My messages stopped yesterday. Not a huge deal, but odd."

"They are doing some upgrades to the ship. Maybe they are upgrading the comm servers."

"That's probably what it is. They had some experimental shielding they were installing."

"Right." Bill started to nibble on my neck. I responded and we made out. That filled up the rest of the evening.

Chapter 9

THE MEETING

August 11, 2169 0745 Hours

I got up and threw on a gym outfit and jogged to my parents' house. I hadn't worked up a sweat yet when I got there and a government hovercraft was already there. I went into the house and Captain Cleveland was talking to my parents. "You're early." He seemed less formal than he was on the call. "Captain Cleveland."
"Dr. Endana Obama."
"Endana?"
"Yes. You are obviously aware of the classified data concerning the Kennedy's mission to Venus?"
"Yes, I was briefed last week. Incredible. I sorry that you couldn't be cured."
I was a little annoyed by that comment. "I'm making the best of it. Shall we sit?"
"Certainly."
"Do my parents need to be here?"
"I'd prefer to speak to you first. Then you can decide what to tell them."
"Okay. Let's go out to the patio." My mother followed us out with a tray of coffee. It was a cooler morning than it had been in a while. I sat down and dabbed myself with a face towel, though it wasn't really necessary. Cleveland sat and thanked my mother for the coffee. He took a sip and pondered his next word. "I understand you know Bill Wallace."

"Yes. We were childhood friends. We would see each other in the summer time here."

"That was when you were still male?"

"Yes."

"Have you had any contact with him now?"

"Yes."

"Are you still close? I mean does he know about what happened to you?"

"We have become reacquainted. He knows me as Endana, now and we have been seeing each other."

"But does he know you were once Darius Obama?"

"What does this have to do with anything?"

"He is a lawyer for the Anti-Space Initiative."

"He does research for them."

"He is their chief counsel."

"What?" For the first time I was unsure of what I heard. "Chief Counsel? Are you sure?"

"They have a battalion of lawyers and Bill Wallace is in charge of them. He didn't tell you?"

"He told me that he was a fact checker for them. He was there to make sure people working at GASA were safe."

"The Anti-Space Initiative is doing everything in their power to shut down space exploration. They have stonewalled a lot of funding and right now and all construction of new starships has been put on hold."

"I can't believe it." I was really mad but also remembered that I kept secrets from Bill too. Still this was a big detail to keep from me."

"So you found out I was with him?"

"Once GASA released all of you, they decided to keep an eye on you, for your protection. After all this time there are still people who wouldn't understand your situation. Or want to."

"GASA's been spying on us? I don't who to be madder at, the Anti-Space jerks or GASA."

"I'm sorry you found out this way. The goal was to not interfere with your lives but to make sure you were able to function the way you wanted to-either as a civilian or a GASA member."

"So what do I do?"

"You're relationship with Mr. Wallace for the time being is still your personal affair, however, if the Anti-Space Initiative continues to interfere with GASA operations, you may be forced to make some difficult decisions."

"I see. Since I am returning to the Kennedy on the 27th, I will try to stay out of trouble."

"I'm sorry, if this upsets you, but we have to protect GASA's interests. Unless, you decide to resign from it, which is your prerogative, we'll expect that you will act with the organization's best interests in mind."

"Oh I will." I wasn't trying to hide my annoyance at all. Cleveland wasn't trying antagonize me but he was doing a good job of it. He got up and bade us farewell. I walked him to the door. He turned to me and said, "I understand you are in a strange position right now. Just tread lightly. If you need any legal assistance-"

I cut him off. "I'll contact your office, thanks." He nodded and left quickly.

I took a few moments to figure out my next move. I sat down at the comm and searched Bill's background. I looked up the Anti-Space Initiative and some of their activities. They are passionate in their beliefs but not a group that I would want a lot contact with. Then I searched their website for Bill. Cleveland was right, with one exception. Bill's personal page did not disparage space travel as much as question it. He posed thoughtful, non-threatening posts and managed to be relatively neutral. Once I was satisfied, I decided to head back to the bungalow. Bill was still working on his briefs. He stopped and came out to the couch. I thought I would be angrier, but I was puzzled. "Hey Babe. How'd the meeting go?"

"It was interesting. Why didn't you tell me you were Chief Counsel for Anti-Space?"

Bill went pale for a moment. Then he took a deep breath. "I didn't want you to think less of me. We never talked shop so I didn't think to correct it. I really do just research stuff."

"You do more than that. You litigate."

"Only when it comes to safety. My superiors know that I have a moderate stance."

"That's a hell of a way to find out, Bill."

"Endy, I didn't want to be a lawyer to you. I'm sorry. I do fight for safety in space, I just do it from the inside. I've lost money because I wouldn't take certain cases."

"All right. Just deal straight from now on, Okay?"

"Deal."

It was a cool night so after a light supper, we went over the fire pit and had cocktails. I rather enjoyed out-drinking Bill. I think he tried to get me drunk a few times but it backfired. So now we just enjoy the drinks and fill moments as much as we can. We started to make out but then he surprised me with a gift. It was a gorgeous dress. "I got your sizes from your wardrobe. I have a tux and tomorrow night we have reservations for Zanzibar in the North End."

"I'm impressed. This dress is amazing and Zanzibar is the most prestigious restaurants in Boston! One thing though-we're not taking the hoverbike, right?"

"Right I have a car. It's not as fast but we can be in the city in an hour."

"Sounds like a date." We continued our make out session.

Chapter 10

MORE MEETINGS AND TOUGH DINNERS

August 14, 2169 1530 Hours

Bill and I decided to get in a day trip to Wellfleet. We brought some bicycles and rode around the beaches and the main street area. I've always enjoyed the simplicity of the area. The Kennedy was state of the art technology for everything, right down to the toilets. It was somewhat refreshing to enjoy a more bucolic environment. Bill liked it too. He said he gets tired of the office pretty fast. That's why he works from home. We stopped for an early dinner. I hadn't had some old fashioned seafood in a long time so we stopped at Moby Dick's for some clams. We were sitting down to eat when a familiar face came up to us. It was Captain Cleveland. "Afternoon, folks." He was casually dressed, and a petite woman, with short, dark hair was with him.

"Cleveland. What brings you to Wellfleet?" I was not happy he was there.

"Believe it or not, I am taking some time off. I'm from Philly and I've never visited the Cape before. Meet my wife, Sasha."

"Nice to meet you." Though he presented her in almost a phony, sarcastic manner, she seemed genuine. "I've heard a lot about you."

"Hello." I really wanted Bill for myself but we both felt a social obligation. "Care to join us?" Bill said it so I wouldn't have to. Sasha was wearing a light linen outfit. "We just love the Cape. I came here a lot as a kid. Phillip here has no idea about real seafood." She seemed nice enough, but the whole situation seemed staged. I couldn't shake the feeling that Cleveland was keeping an eye on us-on me. Bill realized who he was but kept his cool. We were having a nice afternoon (we knew they would be very few) and we didn't want to ruin it. Bill and I looked at each other and silently relented. Sasha seemed genuine enough.

"Where are you from, Sasha?"

"I grew up in Manchester, New Hampshire. Went to college at Babson."

"Nice. I grew up in Aberdeen, Maryland, but we have family and vacation property here on the Cape. Nantucket."

"That's nice."

"So Captain-"

"Please, call me Phillip. We're off duty."

"Okay, Phillip. How long are you on the Cape?

"Well I took two weeks leave, right after I spoke with you and I figured I was already here and Sasha was at her Mom's in Manchester. So we met in Boston and took a shuttle down here."

"Ah. I see." There was a long, uncomfortable pause, then I spoke up. "What do you do for work, Sasha?"

"I'm a biochemical engineer. I own a company in Lexington and we are looking to unlock the genetic codes that produce certain physical traits. We are focusing on birth defects."

"Interesting. Is there an increase in birth defects? I thought they were able to cure most of them."

"Yes, we have come a long way but there is still a great deal of work to do. We are still learning about things at the chromosomal level. Maybe some of your research from the Venus Mission could come in handy." Now I understood Cleveland's angle. He was trying to give his wife an edge. Fortunately, GASA was smart enough to put policies and contractual elements to protect that kind of information. "I'm sure it could but you'd have to go through proper channels. Much of what I do is classified."

"Oh, of course! But I think Phillip can cut through some of that red tape."

"I'm sure he can." I was extremely uncomfortable. Cleveland should have known that discussing classified information in public is expressly forbidden. He's baiting me. As I pondered the next chess move, Bill came to the rescue. He glanced at his watch and said,

"Dear, we have to go, I promised my parents we'd meet them for tennis."

"Oh right. Sorry we have to rush off. We rode bicycles here so it will take some time to get back. Nice to meet you, Sasha."

"Nice to meet you too. Good Luck on your mission."

I smiled as much as I could and we left quickly. We both exhaled when we got outside. "Thanks. I may have wanted to punch them both."

"Yeah, that was really awkward. Fortunately for us my parents are in Europe and I've played tennis once in my life."

"My hero." I planted a long, wet, sloppy kiss on his lips and we held each other for a moment. "We should go before they find us again." We rode back to the car and loaded the bikes. We headed farther down the Cape to Truro and looked around. We didn't go straight back to Nantucket in order to avoid the Clevelands. Our meeting them may have been totally innocent, but I had that feeling in the pit of my stomach that told me something wasn't right.

August 20, 2169 1640 Hours

The next few days were quiet. Nothing odd happened. I spent most of the day going over the new specs for the Kennedy's medical lab. Fascinating stuff. Had dinner with Mom and Dad. Mom was excited for her last Alzheimer's treatment. "I feel like I'm 35 again!"

"Bill and I are really happy for you, Mom." I was relieved. The cure for Alzheimer's was about 30 years old. The cure rate was 99% and the one percent that wasn't cured showed remarkable recovery. This was standard reading at University Medical and quite fascinating.

"You know a century ago they would put Alzheimer's sufferers in nursing homes."

"Those things are so outdated." Dad was upbeat, and relieved that he didn't have to use the homes for Mom. "I saw my dad put his mother into one. He cried for a week."

"Well, with the new science discoveries from space we might eradicate every disease."

"Or find new ones." Bill said quietly, with his face low in his dinner plate. He seemed on edge tonight. We all stopped and looked at him as if he just swore. "Sorry, but it's a possibility." I still have not told him about the Eleusian Virus, or how 230 men fell victim to its gender changing properties. "We know the risks, Bill. We agreed that we'd support that."

"I know. Sorry." He was brooding. I think I knew why. I tried to steer things back to happier subjects. I turned to my mom. "So are you doing anything to celebrate?"

"Your Mom wants to see Europe."

"Really? That will be fun. Any place in particular?"

"I'd like to start in England, Germany, then The New Grecian Republic, The Asian-Czech Provinces, and more."

"Things changed a lot when the EU tanked." I was in med school when all of that happened. It was a political nightmare for Europe and now the European Union was gone due to the gross mishandling of the region economic resources. The Euro failed in a big way and now Europe was slowly building their way back to become a reasonable superpower. The benefit to the US and the rest of the world was that everything was cheap. Flights, lodgings and food; even gift shops were like old timey dollar stores. Elderly Americans were retiring in small villages and living comfortably for pennies on the dollar. "Do you think you buy property there?"

"Maybe. Still love it here though. No place like America."

Bill seemed to perk up. "I drink to that!" Bill held up an iced tea. He hadn't touched alcohol for since the last time we went out drinking. I think he was embarrassed that his girlfriend outdrank him. I was still trying to lighten the mood. "I wouldn't mind seeing Europe. There's a lot of history there."

"You're going into space! You've been to another planet! How impressive is Europe going to be?" Bill was struggling. I looked into his eyes and saw some sadness. He didn't want me to leave and I must say I was having a tough time myself. "Let's go for a walk, Bill." He knew what that meant but he politely excused himself anyway. "We'll be back in a bit."

We strolled out to the patio then onto the beach. It was a cool evening and we saw the end of the sunset where there was the last line of light over the horizon. "I know what you're going to say."

"So, what's going on with you?"

"I think you know."

"Humor me."

"I am having a hard time letting you go. I'm sorry if I ruined dinner.

It's just-"
"What?"
"I'm not sure if I can let you go. I mean, obviously I won't stop you but it's taking every bit of my self-control to not do whatever I can to keep you."
"I love you."
That jarred him. "What?"
"I can't deny my feelings. When you said it before I wanted to say it too, but I was trying not have anything stop me from going into space. The truth is that I loved you from the beginning. I've never been in love before. Not like this."
He hugged me for a long time. We continued in silence for a while, walking and holding each other. We found ourselves at a marina and climbed up onto the pier. We sat and he finally spoke. "Promise me something."
"What?"
"You will marry me when you come back from space."
"Wow, that's a big step. You are willing to wait?"
"I will wait as long as I have to."
"We can make subspace calls. At least within the Solar System."
"Is that a yes?"
"I will think about it. It's just hard to wrap my head around it right now."
"Okay."
Bill seemed okay with a non-answer. Part of me wanted to marry him on the spot. But a strong part of me still wanted to be untethered going into space. I would know better when I was back on the Kennedy. The pull of uncharted space versus the pull of a fulfilling life with someone I love. Damn. This is why GASA wants unattached crew members. I guess if you have someone you aren't truly detached.

August 25, 2169 1010 Hours

I was deciding what to wear to the Governor's Private luncheon. I was ranging from semi-glamourous to full military dress. I figured that I didn't want to stick out so I opted for my day uniform. It was simple clean cut and comfortable. It had enough formality for the Governor without being over the top. I put on simple, basic makeup and styled my hair as if I were reporting for duty. Last night, Bill was still undecided if he was coming. I didn't push the issue, if he wanted to come, it had to be his decision. I finished my makeup and went out to the porch. I pondered my immediate future and hoped the Governor was true to his word. If not, space viruses will be the least of my problems. I got a call on my tablet. It was Tanner. She was dressed in sleepwear and there was someone behind her fixing breakfast. From what I could see it was a shirtless, well-built man. "How are you, Daria?"

"I'm well. Going by Endana these days."

"Right- sorry I remember the name change request. Ready for pre-inspection?"

"As ready as I'm going to be."

"Second thoughts about going back into space?"

"Yes. Let's just say there have been developments."

"I think I can relate. I've had some changes too. Still, I have only been to Mars once and no one has really gone beyond it."

"That's the only thing that's keeping me on board. I just don't want to wonder about it for the rest of my life. I suppose they will declassify Mars someday."

"It will be interesting to say the least. Who knows? Maybe there will be other planets we'll be to travel to."

"Exploration. That's the business we're in, right?"

"Exploration. The loneliest profession."

"We'll be fine. It's only a year, right?"

"Right. Anyway see you in a couple of days."

"Will do."

The screen went dark as I stood up and turned towards the house. I would check with Bill on the way out the front to the car. I got to the couch and my man stood before me, dressed in a business casual outfit and ready to go. I smiled. "Thanks, Bill."

"Anything for you, Babe."

We made good time to the State House on Beacon Hill. We landed at the carport and met the Governor's Assistant, Brian. He was very cordial. "This way, Doctor. Mr. Wallace." He gestured a little more than he had to. He escorted us to a cart and we rode into the State House lobby. "Please go to that elevator over there and it will take you to the Governor's Office."

"Thank You." I said. Brian nodded and drove off in the cart. Bill and I held hands as we walked to the elevator. It was still that old colonial décor so it was dark inside. We rode for less than a minute and entered a large room. Another assistant directed us to the great double doors and they swung open automatically. Standing behind a large, old fashioned wood desk was a tall man, large build and white hair. "Governor Stevens. Hello." We shook hands, and I introduced Bill. They shook hands and the Governor Spoke. "I can't thank you enough for saving my boy."

"My pleasure. I just glad he's okay."

"He's better than okay! He didn't have any direction. He was at college just wasting time and taking up space. Oh, he's a smart kid, just unmotivated."

"So what's changed?"

"You changed him. Now he wants to be a doctor and join GASA! He wants to be a hero like you."

"I just saw an opportunity to help. What kind of doctor would I have been if I let him die?"

"That's the attitude he has now. You not only saved his life, you saved his future. He studies tirelessly now. I have to make him go out with his friends to make sure he has a social life."

"I'm glad I was able to inspire him."

"Is there anything I can do to repay you?"

"I didn't come here for a reward."

"I know. But I'd like to repay you in some way."

"I'm going into space in two days. I guess if you could just make sure my parents, family and friends are taken care of, that would be good. I mean they don't need anything but if something happens-"
The Governor interrupted, "Of Course. Here is my personal number. If you or your family have any problems while you're gone, just have them call."

"Thank you."

"Excellent! Let's eat!"

Chapter 11

THE MARS MISSION

August 27, 2169 0800 Hours

Neither one of us slept really well. Today was the day I was heading back to space. "Can't you wait a few more days?" Bill was not happy.
"Now or a couple of days. It's not going to make much difference. It will just put off the inevitable."
"Yeah." Bill grumbled.
"I could eat one of your famous breakfasts, though."
"Aye, Aye ,Sir!!" Bill smiled and in a sudden comic moment, he leapt out of bed and ran into the kitchen. I got up and set out my work uniform. I packed everything else I was taking; more clothes and makeup than I thought I would. I also packed some trinkets that reminded me of this romantic summer. "Bill, I'm hopping in the shower."
"Okay. Food should be ready by the time you come out."
I washed and used some lotions and scrubbed my hair. I noticed it had gotten fuller and thicker over the summer and I really did nothing to encourage that. I put on my work uniform, did my makeup and spritzed on some of Bill's favorite perfume that he bought for me. I came out and Bill stopped to stare. "I never get tired of looking at you."
"Stop staring and let's eat." Bill set the food down and stole a kiss. I

began to wonder if we could get together one last time before I left. My GASA shuttle was coming for me at noon so we ate and then entertained ourselves.

September 4, 2169 1100 Hours

There's nothing like watching a star ship leave spacedock. Its majesty, its gentleness as it eases out of its mammoth cage is a sight to behold. I don't know of a piece of music that could capture the awe of the event. It was like a ballet with the grace and style of a 5-million-ton ballerina. The USS Kennedy was state of the art when it was built 3 years ago and now it was the most advanced piece of technology mankind has ever created. Since the government released the funding last week, 3 more ships are slated to be finished in the same manner: the USS Solaris, the USS Destare, and the USS Logan. The USS Vonnegut was just finished when the funding was pulled and now it's already orbiting Mars.

I was pleased and very excited with the upgrades to the Kennedy. The medical lab was like a playground for me and I have already completed several experiments that would have taken months in the old lab. I decided I should do full medi-scans of every one assigned to the Kennedy including those of us who were affected by the Eleusian Virus. GASA made sure all of that information was classified. I spent the first few days on board overseeing the decontamination of the ship. We wanted to make sure the male crew members were not affected by lingering viruses. Once I was satisfied with the ship's decon, I met with Captain Tanner and First Officer Felloner. We spent several hours reviewing health protocols and making sure we'd depart for Mars on time. Tanner seemed to be back to her old self, so to speak. She was all business; much of the commander I remember was still in the 5' 10'' brunette. Tanner was statuesque and seemed to be a little more buff. Felloner also seemed all business but gained a bit of sass in her new female, persona. "I will handle the staffing changes." She was laser-focused on the job at hand. "Let me know if you need anything, Doctor."

"Thanks. I will. Any word on the hardware updates?"

"No but I will have Harrison touch base with you later."

"That's fine. Please let me review the list when you are done." She headed towards the bridge to get the staffing issues done. Once

Felloner had sent me the current report, I found it in order. I noticed that about 30 former crew members did not return. About half of them opted for earth assignments and the other ones resigned from GASA. Several good people we lost, not to mention the crew members that Lieutenant Morrison was going to take with her. Several new members needed to be medi-scanned. It was critical to have a healthy DNA imprint of each member, in case we run into any unknown pathogens, or even to grow new tissue in the event of an accident. I had my work cut out for me.

Since we returned from furlough I had not seen much of Harrison. She decided to come back a week early to monitor the ships upgrades. I hadn't been able to accomplish much other than the initial medi-scan after the change. She very dark skinned, darker than me. She graduated top of her astro-engineering class and had the pick of any ship in GASA's small fleet. Harrison was a history buff and chose the Kennedy because of the history of the name. I am actually surprised she didn't visit me on the Cape, knowing that Hyannisport was Kennedy family stomping grounds. As a man, he was competent, stern and lived a very Spartan existence. I only briefly saw him as a woman. She went back home for a weekend and I thought it would be a good idea to check in with her. I called her on the ship's com and a beautiful, well made up face appeared. She was in very good spirits. "Hi Doc! How are ya?" She was uncharacteristically upbeat. "I am doing fine, Telman."
"Oh, I'm going by Terry, now. Have you seen the Engineering section?"
"No, I haven't been down there yet."
"You need to see it! I've made some really great changes!" Harrison briefed us on the computer core updates and some of the new hardware that will help process the Eleusian data faster. She was slender and sinewy. She still had a nice figure, though. "Terry, can you let me know when we can bring the Eleusian drives online? We'll want to start prepping the new labs for continuing research."
"Actually we just finished last night."
Harrison was as tall as she was as a man but curvy. She was still very agile, but definitely full figured. She had lightened her hair to a strawberry blond (it was redder before the gender change).

"Okay. I have a medi-scan in progress. It will take about an hour. I will come down after that."

"Great! See you then!" I noticed some bright colors and artwork behind her as we talked. The medi-scan took a little less time than I thought so I checked the data and went to engineering. I didn't come down here often, but I remembered that it was somewhat drab, Spartan like Telman-Terry used to be. I waited for the lift doors to open and walked out. The drab memory I had of engineering melted away and a flood of pastel colors filled the room. I also noticed plant life intertwined with the new décor and some type of irrigation system to feed them. I walked over the engine core and found three women and two men attending the consoles. A strawberry blond beauty was directing the others. "Terry?"

She turned around and had very glamourous makeup on. "Hey Doc! Looking gorgeous!!"

"Likewise. How was your furlough?"

"It was amazing. Let's go into my office."

We left the area and went into her private office. "I had an incredible time. I never knew being a woman could be so liberating!"

"I understand. I had a surprising time, too."

"I had all these emotions, ideas, things that just never occurred to me as a man. I took an art class and discovered that I love art and color! Fresh flowers! Mosaics! It was like a party in my brain!"

"That's wonderful, Tel-Terry."

"What about you? Why was your vacation amazing?"

"Well. If I tell you, you must keep it a secret."

"I swear."

"I met someone. We fell for each other. Hard."

"I'm so happy for you!" She paused, thinking for a moment, "Isn't that going to make this harder?"

"Yes, but he's willing to wait. I figured I have a year to work out my wanderlust and then, who knows?"

"Well you secret is safe with me."

"Thanks. So I get the new paint job in engineering but what's with the plants?"

"That's an another neat idea I had. I was thinking that the varieties of food we'll be eating is going to get old, and I mean boring pretty quick. The food generator just rearranges the organic soy compound to what we ask; a burger tastes like a burger but it's soy. Since the nutrients are put into the soy matter already we get the nutrients we need but there's a synthetic feel to it."

"But it's all organic isn't it? I mean that's part of the medical department's weekly inspection, to make sure the food base is clean and maintained."

"Yes, and we will still need that. But I did some research and found a way to have fresh vegetables and other organic foods. I even found 3 ways to recycle water while we are in space!"

"That's fantastic! You know, I'm so glad you've found a passion."

"Engineering is still my passion but I've been able to expand some theories to other areas and create some neat stuff."

"Keep me posted, I may need your muse."

"You betcha! There's something else."

"What?"

"I met someone, too. In my art class."

"Is it serious?"

"Kind of. I told him if we still felt the same way in a year then we'd do something about it. Time will tell."

"I'm happy for you."

"Thanks. Catch you later."

"Will do."

I decided to visit the bridge. They were still working on it during the upgrade so I hadn't been up there since. I walked onto the bridge and noticed that it was brighter and a similar color scheme to engineering. The pilot's console was noticeable different as was the med station. I went over to it and fired it up. It took only a moment to download the 100 exabytes of medical data from sickbay. I'd be spending more time on the bridge for future missions. Troy bounced onto the bridge and came over to me. "Hey Doc. How are you?"

"Hey Troy. I'm doing great. How are you? Did you have a good furlough?"

"Sure did. I'm going by Tracy now." She was in her normal work uniform and she looked fresh with minimal makeup. It seems the virus thoroughly feminized all of us.

"Okay, give me time to get used to that. I was going to go by Daria but I had to use Endana. So I am now Endana Obama."

"No middle name?"

"Not yet. Wasn't a high priority."

"I hear ya. Have you seen the Commander?"

"Not since this morning. Did you check the ready room?"

"Not yet. I will see you later." Tracy headed to the ready room. We used to call it a conference room but the Commander, much like several high ranking members of GASA, love that old television show, Solar Missions. Much of the style and verbiage of GASA culture mirrored the language of that show, mostly because of its optimistic view of the future (which is now our present), but also much of its ancient nautical references are still applicable. The ready room was a combination of the Commander's office and a small meeting room. The main conference room was moved to next lower deck. I found Tanner in the shuttle port. "Is everything ready, Doctor?"

"Yes, Ma'am. The medical lab is ready to go, we are about 75% done medi-scanning the new crew members and the sick bay is stocked, computers are updated."

"Excellent." The Commander was pleased. She cocked her head, "Did you see that most of the new crew are men?"

"Yes. I am concerned that they may ask why there are some many women on the ship." I pondered.

"Good point. Well if it becomes an issue, we'll need to tell them truth."

"Okay. One other thing: you must have noticed that our libidos have become very strong."

"Yes, I partied pretty hard on furlough. Harder than I did as a man." Tanner grinned a little, then continued. "The new crewmen may have trouble with super-pheromones. So we will need to be extremely careful."

"I have an idea. I can come up with a compound that can make it easier for us to control our urges. I am still finding useful data from the Eleusian hard drives." I was looking to sink my teeth deeper into that alien data.

"Sounds good. Didn't they integrate them into the ship's mainframe?"

"Troy's, I mean Tracy's idea. Pretty ingenious."

"Tracy! I was hoping she'd use that name. I suggested it." Tanner bubbled. "She and Braddock are working together to blend our system to the Eleusian drives. Oh, and another thing, Braddock didn't change his name."

I was puzzled. "He's going by Jim?"

"No he always preferred Jamie. Said his mother called him that."

"Ah. Makes sense. Well, let me get to work on that compound. Dinner?"

"Sure. Are we dressing for it? It's a habit I developed on furlough." Tanner pondered.

"Let me see how the day goes."

"Okay, see you later." Tanner had fully embraced her womanhood. I guess we all had. I can only imagine who else has boyfriends. "One last thing,"

"What?"

"Did you pick a new name?"

"Certainly did. Deidre."

"Deidre. Nice."

"My friends can call me Didi."

We both smiled and parted. As I headed back to sickbay, I felt a real sense of urgency to develop that compound. I knew that our enhanced bodies could generate an inordinate amount of pheromones. The men, could become aroused to the point of psychosis, if unprotected. I had to work fast.

The first thing I did was increase the amount of oxygen in the ship's ventilation system. I estimated that would work for about twelve hours. I accessed the Eleusian drive and searched for some type of pheromone blocker. I was hoping the Eleusians had run into the same problem and had a ready-made solution. I found something close. It looked like a chemical that could cancel out the pheromones, but it had a highly toxic molecule, close to a barium-mercury hybrid. I had to find a less lethal compound that could be as effective. I decided to get the entire research staff involved. Time was of the essence. I had my original team plus three new members. All top of their class. Two of them were men. I spoke with Tanner and got permission to tell them about the Venus Mission and everything that happened from it.

"You have to be kidding me!" Petty Officer Second Class Neil Case was manly enough. He was understandably shocked. "You used to be a man?"

"Yes. My name was Darius Obama. We found the cure too late for us. Most of us, that I know of, have accepted it and moved on. We had to keep it a secret from the public. Right now as long as an affected person receives the antidote before a month's time they will revert back to normal."

"That's the most incredible thing I've ever heard."

"Well the upside is that we have data from the Eleusians that is far more advanced than anything man has come up with. We have a wealth of knowledge and we'll be spending a lot of time going through it."

Another new crew member, Petty Officer Third Class Harlan Billis, was also surprised. "Ma'am, how many other crew members know this?"

"All those affected, the Captain, Chief Engineer. That's why all the new crew are men. Now listen, all of you: under no circumstances are you to reveal any of what I told you. The survival of everyone aboard the Kennedy depends on it. If anyone asks what you are working on, tell them the projects I've listed on this mission task list."

"Are you asking us to lie, Ma'am?" The third crewman, Seaman John Flowers, was pensive.

"Crewman, I am **ordering** you to lie. As I said, our survival depends on this."

"Aye, Ma'am"

The others returned to their stations and Flowers hung back.

"Something I can help you with, Crewman?"

"Well Ma'am, I joined GASA to explore and experience space. I felt it was an honorable service and I like that about it."

"Go on."

"Well, I'm not sure if I can lie about something like that."

"Consider it classified information. We can't let the population of Earth know that a virus exists that changes their gender. At least until we understand more about it. It just keeps everyone safe. At the very least, it a secret."

"A pretty big one. I will comply, Doctor."

"Very good. Thank you, Flowers." I understand his hesitations. I felt the same way about GASA and the whole reason we are out here.

"Mr. Flowers, if you ever have problems or any issues, feel free to come to me. My door is always open."

"Thank you, Doctor. I may just take you up on that."

Flowers went back to his station and seemed to relax. I didn't like having my people lie about a thing, but there was really no other option. There was still so much about the Eleusians we didn't know. The xeno-archaeology department had months, maybe years of research left on the Eleusian drives. They would be hailed as heroes for just for working on it.

I continued to look for a suitable pheromone blocker compound for the ship. I thought it would take longer, but after only an hour, I found a possible alternative for the toxic elements in the Eleusian formula. Sodium. It had similar molecular bond with the other elements and sodium is palatable to humans. I had to start testing immediately. I need people to test it on and the only one who can authorize that is the Captain. I called Tanner on the com.

"Commander do you have a minute?"

"Sure, Doc. What's up?"

"I've found an element I can use for the pheromone blocker but I need to test it. On a subject."

"Doctor, you know how I feel about human experimentation. My gender may have changed but my beliefs have not."

"I realize that, but this is a critical point. If I can't test the compound, I can't guarantee that the men won't go nuts."

"Is there no other way?" Tanner found any kind of human experimentation abhorrent.

"If I had more time, maybe. By the time we get to Mars the crew will be tearing itself apart, literally."

"All right. Ask for volunteers first. See how you make out and let me know ASAP."

"Aye, Captain."

"Endana,"

"Captain?"

"Be careful. You're the best doctor in the fleet."

"Thanks. I will."

Chapter 12

AN IMPORTANT TEST

September 5, 2169 0800 Hours

The Kennedy was still in orbit around earth. Captain Tanner was waiting for my results before we set off to Mars. Time was of the essence. I needed volunteers and I started with the medical staff. Flowers and Lieutenant Barbara Wilson (formerly Robert), from the xeno-biology section volunteered. Like myself, Wilson was an enhanced female. I got up 2 hours early to prepare the test chamber. I pressurized the tanks with the pheromone blocker and blended the breathable air, matching the normal conditions on the ship. The previous day, the volunteers were instructed to go about their normal routine, both on and off duty. This is to ensure the best possible result under normal conditions. The test chamber would have the normal amount of oxygen, nitrogen and carbon dioxide as if everything were normal. An enhanced female and a normal man together for a few hours should create the proper effect. Flowers brought in some work to do as did Wilson. After an hour, Flowers began to get flushed. He was also looking at Wilson repeatedly. At first, he would steal a glance and then after a while he was staring. "How are you feeling, Flowers?"
"Did the heat get turned up?"
"No. The temperature has not changed."
"Okay. I'm all right."

He continued to work with difficulty and after another half hour he stopped and got up. He wandered around aimlessly then he sat down next to Wilson. He struck up a conversation and they seemed to be just talking. Flowers was sweating a lot and he tried to walk away from her. He went back and she stopped and looked at him. She started to become more interested in him. He noticed that and he began to stroke her hair and she liked it. They were becoming more interested in each other and soon they were kissing. It was then I administered the compound in gaseous form. I started the timer to gauge how long before it took effect. After about 5 minutes they stopped and pulled away from each other. Flowers was embarrassed. "I'm sorry, I don't know what came over me."

"It's okay. It's part of the test. It's actually good that you were affected. If this is successful, we'll be able to live easier knowing the males won't fry their brains."

"I suppose you're right, although it wasn't my brains I was worried about."

"Besides," Wilson smiled wryly, "You're not a bad kisser."

Flowers smiled. That seemed to break the tension. "Thanks, I enjoyed it, too."

I brought both of them out of the chamber and did medi-scans on them. Flowers' pheromone levels were normal as was his mean body temperature. Wilson's level of pheromone output was the same. The compound worked! I informed the Captain and she was ecstatic.

"Administer the compound immediately!"

"I can send it through the ventilation system."

"Do it. I will inform GASA Control that we have solved the problem and that we are ready to head to Mars."

"Aye."

About 20 minutes later, the Captain made an announcement. She sounded the Bosun's Call which is typically used for ceremonial purposes and things of great importance:

"Attention, all hands, this is the Captain speaking. Due to certain important health issues, our voyage to Mars was postponed. I am glad to say that those issues have been resolved and we now have permission from GASA Control to depart for Mars. As of 1130 hours we will be leaving orbit and heading to the Red Planet where we will pick up supplies, receive new crewmen, and drop off some new crew for a new assignment. We will also participate in some research to prepare us for the greatest journey mankind has ever taken. I am proud of this crew, there is none finer, stronger, smarter and better trained. I plan to return in a year with this crew intact and receive a hero's welcome, because I believe that all of you are heroes. May God bless the Kennedy and its crew. Prepare to leave orbit in 30 minutes."

I have heard similar speeches but this one definitely left me with goosebumps. I decided to call Bill. I wanted to see him before we left. Subspace messages will be functional at least while we are still in the solar system. "Hey Babe."
"Hey yourself. You're still in orbit?"
"Yes for another 30 minutes. I just wanted to call you before we left."
"I'm glad you did. I miss you."
"I miss you too."
"Hey look who's here!" Two figures came up behind Bill. It was my parents.
"Hi Mom, Hi Dad! You guys are over Bill's?"
Mom cut in. "Yes we decided to get together every so often until you come back."
"That's nice. I'm flattered."
Dad spoke up. "You guys are real heroes. Everyone wants to hear about your Mars mission."
"I'll report back when we get there."
"I figured you'd be close by now."
"We had some issues to take care of. We're leaving orbit in about 20 minutes."
"Okay, well we'll let you go. We love you! Be safe." Dad was tearing up. I started to, too.
"I will, Dad. I love you, too. I will call when I get to Mars."
"All right, sounds good."
The screen went dark and for the first time in a long time, I felt a little homesick. I shook it off and went to the bridge.

September 5, 2169, 1230 Hours

The Bosun's call sounded again. The commander's voice came over the com:

"All hands, prepare to leave orbit."

The ship took a collective breath and Tanner gave the command. "Engage engines, half-light speed." The bridge was fully staffed and prepared to run the ship. Tanner was in the Captain's Chair; First Officer Tracy Felloner was posted at the Operations Station, the communications officer Ensign Sarah (formerly Samuel) Conway manned comms and Petty Officers Capshaw and Warren were at navigation and propulsion respectively. I was sitting at the bridge medical station and stared at the forward view screen. I glanced at the console and everything was normal. We were on our way. Two planets in less than 6 months. It never really dawned on me that only a short time ago we were finally able to send a man to Mars. Now Mars trips have become routine. It's an administrative trip at best to drop off crew, pick up the rest of our supplies and head to outer space. Once we were moving, I approached the Captain's Chair. "We'll be in Mars orbit in about an hour and a half." Tanner was calm and collected. I was excited enough to lose the homesickness I was feeling earlier. "How long will it take to finish out business there?"
"Not long. Half a day with no issues I suppose." I want to spend as little time there as possible. By the way, I'll need daily progress reports on the status of Eleusian data research."
"Will do, Commander. Are we picking up any more crew on Mars?"
"Not to my knowledge. But there's always a possibility. We'll see what GASA decides."
The trip to Mars was quick and uneventful. We entered orbit in 93 minutes and contacted the Martian Spaceport. Tanner piloted the ship with relative ease. The navigator opened the comms' frequencies as they aligned. We had had audio first. Tanner adjusted in her seat.
"Ensign, hail Mars Command, please."
"Aye, Sir. comms open."
"This is Captain Tanner of the USS Kennedy, requesting permission to enter Mars orbit."
A voice came across the audio. "Please wait while the ship security protocols engage. Identity confirmed. Welcome to Mars, Kennedy.

You may shuttle down at your convenience."

"Thank you, Mars Command." Tanner looked puzzled. "What's wrong?" I was curious.

"We should have visual on the screen. The audio and visual signals are combined in the feed. Why couldn't we see them?"

"We could ping the signal, check the subspace integrity." Conway was checking the comms algorithm. "That should verify the integrity of the signal."

"Would it be effective this close to the planet? Subspace transmissions are used for long distance communication."

"The function algorithms are the same, except for long distances the modulation and power outputs are higher."

"Do it. Let me know what you find."

"Aye, Sir."

Tanner turned to Tracy "I'm probably paranoid, but I want a security detail with every shuttle going to the surface. Something doesn't smell right."

About an hour later, the first ground crew was ready to shuttle to the surface. There were two security officers, 2 from General Science, 2 medical staff (myself included) and 2 bridge crew for administration. Their initial mission was to secure the supplies we needed for deep space and make contact with Mars Command. Normally, we would download all collected data to the Archives, but we had to encrypt everything concerning the Eleusians and the Venus Mission. Tanner was leery about letting that information out; fortunately, our data research team was able build solid encryptions and dummy algorithms to boost the firewalls and shield the data from wandering eyes. Tanner arranged that the data be the last thing we deal with and then make a hasty exit. I agreed.

The shuttle landed on the pad and a crew was waiting for us. A tall, dour looking man walked up to us and introduced himself. "I am Chief Petty Officer Wesley Barton and I am going to be handling you resupply operations."

"I am Dr. Obama. This is Lieutenant Wilson, my assistant. We will be handling the medical supplies while my colleagues will handle everything else."

"What about those two?" Barton was all business.

"They are security. Just a precaution for any Anti-space sentiment." I was trying to mask their true reason for being here.

"This is highly unusual. Who would travel to Mars and be anti-space?"

"I hear ya, but Captain's orders."

Barton was offset. "Very well. He turned on his heels and walked into the hangar bay. I clearly outranked him but this was his domain. I decided to remain diplomatic, knowing how anxious Tanner and the rest of the Kennedy crew were about being here. We followed Barton into the vestibule then the main corridor. He stopped and turned around. "The labs and quartermaster are that way," he pointed to the left. "Sickbay and medical supply are that way. You are free to take advantage of any part of the facility, barring the classified areas. They are marked by the red and yellow hash-marked stripes. Please do not try to access them without permission."

I was curious. "Why do you have classified areas?"

"We have several, highly sensitive experiments going on and we need them to remain undisturbed."

"Okay. We aren't going to be here too long. Captain's anxious to get out there."

Barton grunted. "Hmm. Well I let you get to it then. Contact me on the station comms if you need anything. I am on duty until 1800 hours." Barton excused himself and walked off towards the operations center. "That guy creeps me out." Wilson was put off by him.

"Yeah, me too. Maybe he's been on Mars too long. Anyway let's get to work. I want to get out of here as soon as possible."

The next couple of hours went smoothly as we loaded several storage containers to be sent up to the Kennedy. We met with Barton at 1545 hours, to clear the station and prepare to load the Eleusian data into the Archives. During the download, the current archive would also be uploaded so we would have all the information from the Martian database. Barton met us at the Archive Upload Port to assist us. He had a data card as did we. Our security protocols were contained on the card, and both cards had to be inserted into the com port console in the Archive to initiate the data exchange. Once it began it could not be stopped; any attempt to stop or interrupt the process would trigger a complete data dump in order to protect the station, not to mention GASA interests. Barton inserted his card and I inserted mine. We started the process and waited for a few minutes. Small talk with Barton was next to impossible.

"So, where are you from?"

"Minnesota," he responded mechanically.

"Must be cold."

"Mmm."

I thought I might try a bit of an experiment. I suspected that I might be able to control the level of pheromones I radiated so I thought I would try to flirt with Barton to see if I could get a rise out of him. I moved in closer to him and he squirmed a little. I dropped my voice just a little and looked at him. He met my gaze and acted a little shy. I pouted a little. "It must get lonely here."

He broke the gaze and moved away. "I have a partner here. We're very happy."

"You mean like work partner?" I was purposely playing a little dumb.

"We work and live together."

"That's good. It's not good to be alone out here."

"GASA thought the same so they allowed us to bring partners or spouses. He was already in GASA so it was easy to get assigned together."

"Your partner is male?"

"Yes." Barton was smitten and moved closer to me.

"That's too bad." I decided I had tortured him enough and moved away. I returned to my professional demeanor. Barton snapped out of it but he was a little thrown. I looked at the console and saw that the data exchange was synced. "It's done. We'll initiate the classified data next."

"O-okay." Barton was snapping out it but my quick experiment was a success. I didn't want to overwhelm him but I was able to gain his interest despite the fact he was gay. It was a fascinating development and I decided I would later isolate the pheromone for further study. In the meantime, I felt it would have been cruel to push Barton any farther.

I contacted the Kennedy and requested the encrypted download. We together initiated the process and it was significantly shorter. I kept my distance from Barton but he would steal glances every so often. I wondered if I had gone too far. I turned to him. "Are you okay?"

He stammered a bit. "You seem to have an unusual effect on me."

"How so?" I decided to play dumb again.

"When you were close to me, I felt-"

"Felt what?" I knew what he felt.

"Attracted to you. I've never been attracted to a woman, any woman for that matter. It's a new experience."

"I'm flattered." I felt bad I messed with Barton's head. It was a mistake. "Do you know why you feel this way?"

"No. It's like I've been drugged. It's a very strange sensation."

"Well I am a doctor, I could check you out?" That sounded horrible.

"No, I think I should go to the infirmary for a checkup. Thank you." Barton turned to leave and I wanted to apologize because I knew it was my fault, but it would compromise the Eleusian data, not to mention our entire mission. I had to live with that. "Take care, Mr. Barton."

"Safe travels, Doctor." Barton walked out of the port room. I hoped the best for him and I endeavored to get to the truth about the Eleusians and this condition they left us in. I met the ground crew to do a quick debrief and return to the Kennedy. I reported in and recorded our activity without mentioning my informal experiment with Barton. I hope I didn't ruin him.

September 5, 2169 1730 Hours

We took off from the pad and headed up to the Kennedy. As we rode, there was a faint sound like a distant thunder. I looked out the shuttle window and saw that half of the Mars Command Center was blown out and people were scrambling to get to the escape pods.

"Turn Around!" I commanded. Wilson was piloting the shuttle and responded immediately. "Send a distress call to the Kennedy. We need medical and engineering for triage and disaster recovery!"

"Aye Sir!" Wilson was an expert pilot and put the shuttle down to the damaged area. "Oxygen suits!" Wilson pressed a button on the console and the emergency closets opened. All of us trained for this so we all donned suits and marked ready. Wilson was the pilot but I was the senior officer in charge. "Deploy!" Wilson punched the airlock control and all the air rushed out of the shuttle. We bounded out to render assistance. "First priority is secure the personnel!" I screamed. Everyone, including the security detail scrambled to grab the choking people. We moved as fast as we could. I grabbed a shirtless male and dragged him into the working airlock. It was fortunate that explosion happened near multiple airlocks. I pulled him in and hit the decompression switch. When I rolled him over, I saw that it was Barton. He was unconscious but alive. I administered an oxygen push to supply his cells with oxygen. He came to with a start. I took off my helmet and calmed him down. His skin was red due to bursting capillaries. He coughed and gasped for air and when he could he spoke. "Explosion in Archive. Last download-virus-tried to remove it-created a feedback loop. "

Barton struggled and then passed out from his injuries. I brought him to the infirmary, which was not damaged in the explosion. From a quick check he would be okay. I felt a twinge of guilt as I turned to leave the infirmary. I went back to Barton who was in and out of consciousness. "I am so sorry Barton. For everything." He seemed to have heard me so I kissed him on the cheek and left. I rushed out to the airlock and peered through the window. There were body parts floating and teams containing plasma fires. The recovery system sealed the hole but several crew were assisting in making sure it was a good seal. The Martian climate is a harsh one. I put my helmet back on and shut the airlock. I had about 2 hours of air so I went outside to investigate. The northeast wing of the complex had a twenty-foot hole in the wall and roof. What was left of the data core hung apart like a carcass that blown out from the inside. The computer operations system seemed to remain undamaged. The wall seal was a like balloon like mass that sealed the hole as it expanded. The crew held it by cable until it seated in place. They applied the corbomite sealants and secured the barrier. Once secured, air was pumped into the room to make it habitable. Emergency protocols required that we remained in our space suits with ample air supply in case of a breach. The shuttle crew met in the data core room.

"Is everyone accounted for?"

"Yes, Ma'am. All the crew is here."

"Okay, what happened?"

Wilson stepped up. "As far as we can determine the source of the explosion was the core."

"The core?"

"Yes, Ma'am. About 65 minutes after we uploaded the classified data, the core went critical and exploded, blowing out this section of the wall." Wilson gestured towards the sealed wall.

"What do the scans show?"

"Nothing abnormal, at least until," Wilson paused.

"Until what?"

"An attempt was made to access the classified data."

"Was it authorized?"

"That's the weird part. The user was authorized but the security prompts failed."

"Failed? They were working fine before we left."

"There was one odd thing, an anomaly if you will, that was detected before the explosion."

"What was it?"

"A psionic pulse. Whoever tried to access the data, got a brain blast from the computer."

"That's not possible! We've barely scratched the surface of psionic science."

"There is one clue. Not sure if it's even that. The pulse left an image on the screen."

"Were you able to capture it?"

"Yes, it's pretty much burned into the screen. It even left bumps." Wilson pulled out her pad and showed me. It was an alien language. One that anyone who visited Venus a few months ago and was changed could read. Wilson was discreet when she didn't reveal that she and I, could read it. It said in Eleusian language, "The Battle continues, long live the Eleusian Revolution."

Wilson and I looked at each other, not really knowing what to say. I spoke up. "We'll need to report this to the Captain."

September 6, 2169 0110 Hours

"You're sure you read it right?" Didi was in her night clothes. She had kept abreast of what was happening with the shuttle crew. She was looking at the image of the screen. I was really exhausted but I wanted to show it to her in person. "I've shown it to several of us and they all said it said the same thing."

"Yeah, that's what I see too. How the hell did this happen?"

"We don't know. Science is checking the Eleusian drives and searching for anything that might provide a clue."

"Do me a favor. Get the xeno-historians in on this. I want to know what was going on with the Eleusians when things went south in their society. That information may prove just as useful."

"Aye, Sir."

"Also make sure your shuttle crew gets some rest. It's been a long day. They can report to duty at noontime tomorrow. Give them the morning to rest. More if they need it."

"Thank you, Captain."

"It's after hours, Doctor. You can call me Didi."

"Good night, Didi." She smiled when I said her name. I needed that.

I slept pretty well. I decided to take the morning off and rest. I caught up on some reading and got a massage. I wanted to check in with Tanner at noontime and she agreed. I wrote a few letters, to my parents and Bill. I had a late breakfast and started toward the Captain's Quarters. I pondered our next move. I met Tanner outside her quarters. Under normal circumstances, we would have left orbit by now. I suspected that due to the accident, the Captain consulted with GASA and they had us wait and conduct a full investigation.

"Stuck here for a while, are we?" I tried to lighten her mood.

"Yes," she grumbled. "Full investigation, the whole nine yards. Damn, I wanted to get out of here."

"I know. Me, too." Tanner had her hair down and styled. "How is your friend, Barton?"

"He's stable. Once he's able to talk without difficulty, we should ask him questions."

"Right. Who else was down there?"

"Most of the staff was off-duty. The crew quarters were on the other side of the complex so casualties were minimal."

"But we lost some?"

"Yes. Four. Once the bodies are retrieved, we will do full autopsies."

"Do you know what happened?"

"I sent you the brief and the shuttle crew statements."

"Danna, (she started calling me that) What happened, really? You were there."

"We were already in the shuttle when the explosion happened. Somehow the archive core exploded."

"Why, in your opinion?"

"I have no idea, but,"

"But what?"

"I think it has to do with the Eleusian drives."

"The data? What kind of data causes an explosion?"

I pondered. "The alien kind."

Tanner walked over to the bay window. "I don't understand."

"The only thing that was unusual about the download was the Eleusian data. It has to be connected."

"How long until we know for sure?"

"No way of telling."

"Damn. The last thing I wanted to do is spent a lot of time here."

"I know but GASA won't let this go. They'll want answers."

"All right. Start an investigation-coordinate with Ship Security and get this thing buttoned up."

"Aye, Ma'am."

"Danna, I want to be kept abreast of the investigation. Before GASA if possible."

"You got it."

"Thanks."

I nodded and Tanner headed towards the bridge. I figured I should inventory the data and check the drives that we uploaded to the Mars core. I contacted Wilson and we went to the Computer Science Lab. We brought up the logs and poured through exobites of the Eleusian data. After about an hour of finding nothing unusual, I broke for a cup of coffee. When I came back I continued viewing the logs. After about 10 minutes, I discovered an anomaly in the encrypted data stream. "Are you seeing this?" Wilson looked over at my screen. "Yeah, I see it."

"What could it be?"

"It's a repeating pattern. It seems familiar."

"It sounds familiar to me too."

Together it seemed like the pattern was saying something to us. We both sounded it out:

"Beware the strands, the result will destroy!"

Wilson and I couldn't believe that we understood it.

"That's what it said, right?" Wilson was stunned.

"Yes. I suspect that it's another benefit to being an enhanced female.

We need to report this to the Captain."

"Shouldn't we tell security first?

"Let me brief the Captain then you can brief security. She wanted to know first."

"Is that kosher? I mean security should really have the first briefing, shouldn't they?"

"Normally yes, but with the Eleusian data, it's an unusual situation and also highly classified. I know all the security staff has clearances, but some of the new crew, male crew may not understand. Until we have more pertinent information, we should brief the Captain first."

"Yes, you are correct, Doctor."

I contacted Tanner on secure comms. She was on the bridge. "You need to be alone for this."

"Okay." She had the comms transferred into her study and sat down. "What's the latest?"

"We found an anomaly in the Eleusian data stream. The last one we sent through the core."

"Okay, so what did you find?"

"It was a pattern inside of the data. Wilson confirmed that it was a message."

"From who?"

"I am pretty sure it was a warning from the Eleusians. We were able to sense it."

"Sense it?"

"Yes. The Eleusian Effect has given us a sixth sense when it comes to the data.

"Is that what we're calling it now?"

"Keeps it simple. Anyway due to our enhanced bodies, and now I guess our enhanced minds, we seem to have some mental connection to our benefactors from Venus."

"Let me see it."

I took my pad and paired it with Tanner's console. The anomaly flashed on the screen and Tanner looked at it and nodded as if she understood it. "What do you think they meant by 'the strands'? Could they be referring to DNA strands?"

"We think so. Everything the Elcusians have done as far as bio-information management has been at the genetic level. Their tech has bridged the digital to the biological and we are still learning about that bridge."

"What about the autopsies? I want them done here on the Kennedy."

"Affirmative. The facilities on Mars were damaged so we have little choice. I will have the bodies brought on board, immediately."

"Very good." Tanner paused for a moment.

"Is there something else commander?"

"I know I said that I wanted to leave Mars as soon as possible but we need to find out what killed those people. I won't have the deaths of four people hovering over my head while I'm commanding this ship in deep space."

"I will be thorough. I want to know as badly as you do."

"Keep me posted."

"Aye."

"I hate to have you pull an all-nighter, but we need to get this wrapped up as soon as possible."

"I understand. I probably wouldn't have slept much anyway."

I left Tanner's room and went to the shuttle bay. I contacted the mortuary detail and had them prepare an empty lab to store and study the casualties. It would take about an hour to transport the cadavers up to the morgue, so I went to the cantina and got some coffee.

Wilson was there waiting for the shuttle. "I thought you went to bed."

"Couldn't sleep. I need to know what happened to those people."

"Me too. I'm doing the autopsies when they get here. Want in?"

"Absolutely. Maybe it will shed some light on what the Venusians did to us."

"Maybe so." Wilson's comment struck a chord. "Why don't you take that angle?"

"What do you mean?"

"Well, once we do the autopsies, we can study that strand and weird message. Find out why we could read it so easily."

"Yeah. I will be happy to solve that mystery."

"It's settled. So how are you adjusting?" I pretty much knew the answer, but I figured I'd make conversation.

"I'm fine. Actually better than fine. On furlough, I ran a marathon and raised some money for charity."

"Wow, that's great. I just vacationed with my parents."

"Whereabouts?"

"Cape Cod. We have a summer home there."

"Can I ask you a question?"

"Sure"

"Did a Captain Cleveland come and see you?"

"Yes!" I was very surprised.

"He came and saw me, too. I didn't know what to say, I just told him who I was. He seemed to already know."

"Catching people off guard seems to be his specialty. He got me twice. Used his wife to try to get some additional information out of me. I was surprised at such a transparent attempt."

"Same here. The second time I was with my brother and we were boating out on Lake Powell."

I got even more curious. "Did he have his wife with him?"

"As a matter of fact he did."

"What did she look like?"

"She was gorgeous. Very tall, taller than him, long blond hair, slender face and build."

Interesting. What was her name?"

"Elaine."

"Not Sasha?"

"No, definitely Elaine."

"I knew something didn't smell right with him. He working some sort of angle. He wants something from us. Something having to do with the Venus mission."

Wilson was pensive. "I thought that too."

"Did either of them say what his wife did for a living?"

"Something in bio-engineering. Some biotech company in Denver."

"Said the same for his east coast wife, 'Sasha'. He's either a bigamist or he's trying to get some information from us."

"Who is this guy? Why is he trying to con us?"

"I don't know. But as soon as this Mars business is done, I am going to find out."

Chapter 13

REQUIEM

September 9, 2169, 0214 Hours

The bodies had finally arrived and I got to work. Wilson and I started together, doing the first body. Once we finished, she started her part of the investigation. I spent four hours on autopsies and finished the basic scans. I decided to nap for an hour and check in with Wilson after. She hadn't taken a break since we started. I supposed I could have kept going but I wanted fresh eyes when I saw Wilson's findings. When I saw her data, I was glad I took the nap. I met her in the Genetics lab. "What's you find?"
Wilson was offset. "You aren't going to believe this."
"Try me."
"Well I was able to isolate the anomaly and compared it to several patterns. Genetic, cellular, binary, hell I even tried music."
"So what happened?"
"It changed."
"Changed? How?"
"The message was different. Every time I tried to isolate the pattern, the pattern changed, almost like it was trying to communicate."
"So the data stream was sentient?"
"Not quite. There were repeating patterns in the anomaly."

"But you said that you ran several patterns against it? How do you know?"

"Well, being an enhanced female has more benefits than we discovered."

"You mean you could just read it."

"Yes."

"We have to find a non-enhanced way of publishing this data. Do you think you can find some kind of filter that allows normal people to process this information?"

"I honestly don't know."

"I have an idea. The Eleusians were able to use genetics to code technical data. I think the answer may be genetic."

"But like I said I ran…." Wilson stopped in mid-sentence. "How stupid of me! I was running normal, unchanged DNA against the anomaly! I need to use the DNA of an enhanced person! The easiest way is a blood sample."

"I was thinking the same thing. Let's check the DNA records of 10 enhanced and 1 non-enhanced as a control. Randomize them."

"I will get right on it."

"I will contact the Captain and update her. I will check back in a couple of hours."

"Roger that, Doc."

I went to the com and called Tanner. She was sleeping but expected regular updates. She took a moment and answered. "Captain, I have an update."

"Sure, go ahead."

"The anomaly pattern changes. It says other things when we apply energy. It's not sentient but it's trying to tell us something."

"What else is it saying?"

"Wilson says it's like it trying to contact someone. Or something?"

"Like a distress call?"

"Possibly. We're not sure yet. We figured that the pattern didn't follow any known combinations. We've theorized that the pattern was genetic, but not a normal DNA sequence."

"What do you mean?"

"Wilson tried a normal human genome pattern and was unsuccessful so we are trying one from an enhanced human."

"One like us?"

"Yes."

"Excellent work, Doctor. Please tell Wilson the same."

"Will do."

"Tanner out."

I went back to the morgue to finish the autopsies. There was a message for me on the com. It was from Barton. He was conscious and wanted to speak with me. I returned the message and I would shuttle down tomorrow to see him. As I was curious as to what he had to say I turned my focus back to the autopsies. With Wilson working on the anomaly pattern, I made swift work of the exams. All 4 persons were men and died of trauma caused by extreme decompression and exposure to the Martian atmosphere. In other words, once they were blown out of the station, the absence of pressure and breathable air ripped their lungs apart. The natural atmosphere of Mars was acrid and toxic. Fortunately, any suffering by these men in death was quick. I took special care to craft the exam reports, along with official death certificates. I also made funeral arrangements to take place on the Kennedy and briefed the Captain. I thought that it was important to get some background information on them so I decided that when I saw Barton, I would gather some personal information on the deceased.

September 10, 2169 0730 Hours

I decided to get a full night's sleep so, I woke up refreshed. I scheduled a shuttle trip to Mars Station and asked Wilson to come with me. We landed just after 0830 and met with Commander Richards. He was cordial and easy going.

"Mr. Barton is anxious to see you."

"I can imagine. How is he?"

"Recovering well enough."

"Well enough?"

"Well there has been significant changes in his DNA structure. The changes are actually healing him, making him healthier at a rapid rate."

"That's interesting. Good I guess."

"Yes but it is also raising the level of estrogen in his system. It's like he contracted a virus and it's turning him female."

"That's incredible!" I couldn't let on that I knew why this was happening to poor Barton. The good thing is that we developed the cure. I had to figure out a way to get it to him before we left orbit.

"May I see him? He asked to see me."

"Certainly. This way."

We walked to the infirmary and past the damaged area. I walked to a curtained area and behind it was Barton. He looked much better than the last time I saw him. His hair was significantly longer, and his features were softer. He had lost that hatchet demeanor and seemed shorter though it was hard to determine with him lying in bed. Standing next to him was a large man, crew cut and in uniform. I figured this was his partner. He was holding hands with Barton.

"How are you, Mr. Barton?" I made sure to use my most professional bedside manner. It was my fault Barton was in this mess. "I am on the mend, Doctor. As matter of fact I feel great. They said I healed faster than anyone on record."

"That's excellent. I guess there's little work for me here. What did you want to see me about?"

"I wanted to say I'm sorry."

"Sorry? For what?"

"Reacting the way I did before the accident. When we were doing the data sync."

"You didn't do anything wrong."

"I'm afraid I made you think I was interested in you. I should have done that."

"It's okay. I didn't think that at all." I felt like crap.

"The other reason I wanted to talk to you is that before you came down, we received a signal. A most unusual signal."

"Why tell me? I can have Lieutenant Wilson look into that."

"Yes you should but it was most unusual. You see we sensed it." This sounded familiar. "Sensed it?"

"Yes. It was like our minds were the receivers. Like comms."

"Okay I will look into that. You said, 'we'?"

"Everyone on the station, almost everyone."

"Who didn't?"

"The women."

"Hmm," I was trying extremely hard not to let on that I knew much more about this situation. "I will see what I can find out."

"Oh, I am sorry. I didn't introduce my partner. Doctor, this is Chief Petty Officer Sean Parker, my domestic partner."

We shook hands. "Mr. Parker. Did you receive the message too?"
"Yes, but mine was somewhat muddled."
"How so?"
"I heard something but, I couldn't understand it. Not like Philip could."
"Interesting. I will look into it."
"Thank you doctor." Barton's demeanor was significantly softer.
"I'll check back on you before I leave."
Barton nodded and I shook Parker's hand left the infirmary. A backup data core was set up and most of the archives had been restored. I decided that another update of Eleusian data was a bad idea so I restored the data lost (downloaded from the Kennedy) and started to research the dead crew members.

1. Ensign Richard Dellworth. Satellite Research Manager
    a. Originally from Washington, D.C, comes from a well-to-do family that is politically connected. Father-Walter Dellworth, Cabinet staffer, mid-level. Mother, Madison Collston, socialite, family socially connected in New York, with business connection abroad. Born second child out of four, has two brothers and a sister. Decided to enter GASA to bolster future political aspirations. Has bachelor's in Computer Science with concentration in space communications
2. Ensign James Stophler, JR. Logistics Manager
    a. Originally from Detroit, Michigan. Family is middle class. Father, James Stophler, SR., a Master Aircraft Technician for Galactic Air. Mother, Linda Redmond, nurse at Detroit Memorial Hospital. Born youngest of three, has two older sisters. Excelled at math and science in school, has bachelor's in both Mechanical and Electrical Engineering.
3. Chief Petty Officer First Class Devan Franklin, Tactical Programming Specialist
    a. Originally from Dorchester, Mass. Upper middle class family, socially prominent parents. Father, Donald, is a minister, large church at the Tremont Temple in Boston. Mother, Beatrice, is the church business

manager. Born third of six children, he has two brothers and three sisters. Father is local alderman with political aspirations to state legislature.
4. Crewman Louis Frenchette, Base Facilities Specialist
  a. Originally from Montreal, Canada, joined GASA after a horrible car accident which claimed the lives of his entire family. Father, Jacques Frenchette, deceased, doctor of internal medicine, Mother, Annette Williams, deceased, biologist, geneticist. One brother, Jacques, Jr., deceased, college student. Details are few on the fatal vehicle accident that claimed the lives of his family. Louis was spared only because he was too sick to go to the holiday party held by Annette's company, Randor Biotech . In a strange turn of events, two months after the tragic event, the company closed permanently, and all of its assets, proprietary data and money disappeared. There was no investigation into the company and the investigation of the accident was wrapped up quickly and quietly. Louis has no next of kin on record.

I was saddened when I read about Louis. It would be difficult to make arrangements with no next of kin. I would solve that problem last. My somber task was interrupted by a crewman who attending Mr. Barton. "Doctor! Come quick, it's Barton!"
"What's happened?" My sadness turned to dread as I ran to the infirmary. What have I done to poor Barton? I came in and he was writhing in pain. I recognized the changes and forgot that I was supposed to keep my knowledge of this situation classified and quiet. "Quickly, roll him over and level the bed!" I commanded. I found a muscle relaxant to ease Barton's pain as he makes his final gender change. "This should ease the pain."
Parker was there and worried. "Is he going to be all right?"
"I'm doing my best. He seems to be coming out of it." Barton's pain subsided and he calmed down. I knew I had to get him the antidote before too long, but the question remains: What caused Barton to change gender? We knew what changed us but this was a new development. Would our antidote work? Was I somehow to blame for Barton's affliction? More questions related to the Eleusian Effect.

I hope we can fix this before it gets worse.

Barton was resting comfortably. I asked Parker what happened. "We were talking and he was feeling pretty good, and then he got really hot."

"Hot? Like a fever?"

"Yeah, I guess. I could feel the heat from him and then he was in a lot of pain."

"Does he have a current medi-scan? I'll need to check it."

"Yes we just had our 6 month scan."

"Okay, stay with him."

"There's something else."

"What?"

"He's changed.

"How?" I already knew.

"He's not fully male anymore."

I had to make it sound convincing. "I'm sorry?"

"He's turning female."

I tried to look incredulous. "How do you know?"

"He had me feel his body. He seemed confused but not in distress. He is growing breasts and his hips are widening, like a woman."

"That's not, possible." It was hard to keep up the act.

"Well, his genitals are not the same. He asked me to feel them and I said he should have the doctor or a nurse do that but he was scared. He didn't know what to do. So I looked and he barely has anything there."

"Okay, let me look at his scan and figure out what's going on." I knew I had to report this to Tanner right away. I knew the station monitored all comms so I needed either a secure channel or see her in person. I decided that I would try a secure line. Tanner appeared on the com screen. "We have a situation." I tried to be as succinct as possible.

"What happened?"

"It's Barton. He's changing." Fortunately, Tanner also understood the need for discretion, even on a secure line. "How?"

"Seems like he is developing female characteristics. We don't have all the data yet."

"Keep me posted. Tanner out."

She knew that we would continue this conversation later. Right now I went back to the infirmary and Barton was still transitioning. I wasn't as alarmed as the others. I passed it off as an inherent medical instinct but I knew what we were dealing with and I was confident that we could cure him. Right now, I needed to assist Barton through his changes. After a few minutes and several cc's of sedative we got him calmed down. I figured I would shortcut this whole thing and call it an alien genetic infection. I went back to the Kennedy and retrieved the antidote we developed. It was untested since no one since the Venus Mission had been exposed to the Eleusian virus like we were. I got Tanner's support to test it on Barton. We altered the data as it was reported to Mars Command and prepared to administer it. I was gone a full 24 hours from the Mars station when I got a personal call from CPO Parker. "Doctor, can we meet before the procedure? I need to talk to you-it's urgent."

"Certainly, Mr. Parker. I will meet you in the control room conference area at 0800 hours."

"Thank you. Parker out."

I was curious and concerned about what Parker needed to discuss. Still, I went ahead with all the preparations for Barton's treatment.

September 13, 2169 0745 Hours

I shuttled to the Mars Station and headed towards the conference room to meet with CPO Parker. My curiosity was peaked and I was anxious to hear what he had to say. I dropped off the treatment apparatus for Barton and had the med-techs set things up. I went to the conference room and sat down. My wait was brief as Parker walked in almost immediately. He closed the door and we sat at the enormous table.

"Good morning, Doctor."

"Good morning, Parker. What's this all about?"

"I'll get right to the point. We do not want the procedure."

"'We'? You mean you and Barton?"

"Yes."

"Why?"

"Let me show you." Parker activated his wrist com. "Come in."

The doors slid open and a gorgeous, vaguely familiar female walked in. "Hello Doctor. How are you?"

"I'm fine. Have we met?" I said that with a rock in the pit of my stomach.

"It's me, Barton."

I had to look surprised. Barton was stunning with just a hint of the man I had met a few days ago. "How are you feeling?"

"Good. Great, actually. Except, now I am now a woman."

Parker spoke up. "This is why I wanted to talk to you. I, we, wanted to know if this is permanent if left untreated."

"Well this is uncharted territory. We will need to run tests." I already knew the answer to that question.

"I understand. This is very ironic. You see Philip was looking to transition to female in a few months."

"I see."

"He had started hormone therapy last week. We were expecting to spend a year working on his transition and then have the final surgery."

"So he was planning to become female anyway?"

"Yes. So this has been an unexpected blessing."

"Let me guess. You want to stay female, so you are refusing the treatment?"

"We would like to take advantage of this, 'event', but we need some questions answered first."

"I think I can help. Fire away."

The couple looked at each other somewhat puzzled, but continued. Philip spoke first. "Is it permanent?"

"Well I can only tell you what we've discovered so far-also it is classified. You are not to discuss it with anyone other than me."

"Understood." Barton took over the questioning. I continued

"If left untreated for 30 days, then it is permanent."

"Why 30 days?"

"After that your genetic structure is locked. The DNA become unchangeable."

" Is there a risk of staying this way?"

"No. Your body will actually be stronger, your mental acuity is magnified and your sex drive is tripled."

"Wow!" Parker was understandably impressed.

"You are basically an enhanced human. Even your reproductive organs are completely altered. You'll be able to have children."

"That's incredible! There's no downside!"

"Well actually, your pheromone production is 9.2 percent stronger than any normal female. You will have to be careful who you interact with. Most men, with prolonged contact with you will have issues and eventually become mad with passion."

"There aren't too many people up here. That shouldn't be too much of a problem."

"Nevertheless, you must use the pheromone blocker that I have included in the treatment protocol. It will have to be modified for individual use. Not that you need to use a lot of it in your quarters, but you may want to have some handy if you want to get anything done."

"We can have our own children?"

"Yes, but wait for a while until your body and mind adjust to each other. Your mind will change; you will look at things differently. You will become totally female in mind, body and spirit. After the 30 days there is no going back. Consider this carefully."

"Doctor," Barton was almost in tears, "I have wanted this my whole life. I don't think I would change my mind in 30 days."

"I understand, but you should know all of your options. I am going to set up the treatment so you can self-administer, if necessary. Have the med-techs handy just in case. Also, if you have family, you should contact them immediately and tell them what's happened. In your case it should not be difficult, since you were going to transition anyway."

"We will. Thank you, Doctor."

"Mr., excuse me, Ms. Barton, have you chosen a name yet?"

"Yes, Sheila, after my grandmother."

"Excellent. I will include this in my report. Make sure you file the proper security forms with GASA. I need you to remember one more thing. We don't know why this happened or how; myself or someone else from GASA may need to study you and your condition. Be careful. I would keep this under wraps for now. Do not draw too much attention to yourselves."

"Count on it, Doctor. We are grateful."

I spent two hours reconfiguring the treatment protocols but it was just an obligatory task. I didn't think Barton would change her mind and in a way I was glad, mostly because it salved my conscience. Plus, I hope they will be happy.

I was back on the Kennedy and called Tanner. We met at 1030 hours and I told her everything.

"Still though, how did it happen?"

"That may be my fault. I did an informal experiment on Barton."

"What did you do?"

"I literally turned on my charm."

"Say, what now?" Tanner put her coffee down.

"I theorized that I could control my level of pheromone output at will. I honestly didn't think it would make any effect. I was wrong."

"What happened?"

"I flirted pretty hard with Barton. I knew he was gay so I figured I was safe. I suspect I turned it on so hard, I affected him with the Eleusian Effect via pheromones."

"Holy Crap, Danna! Can you imagine the damage you could unleash on an unsuspecting person?"

"Yes, Didi, I felt horrible about it after."

"You cannot breathe a word of that to anyone! If it got out that we enhanced women could control people like that, I'm afraid the temptation for some may prove too strong."

"You and I are the only ones."

"Okay, well this ends it."

September 18, 2169 0800 Hours

A few days had passed and I had finished the eulogies for the victims of the explosion. I was going to meet with Captain Tanner so she could deliver it. Family members of three victims traveled to Mars and met on the Kennedy for a military funeral. All the families were given the option to have their deceased loved ones buried in space with full military honors. Only Louis Frechette had no family on record. Poor man. I felt bad and somewhat responsible for his death. He will be committed to the vast nothingness of space. I thought of Bill. I haven't spoken with him for a while and now with the burial of the Mars victims, we would be cleared for deep space. I decided I would put in a subspace call before we left orbit.

I entered the assembly chamber. The service was brief but adequate. For the first time since we changed genders, Tanner looked uncomfortable. She tugged at her uniform when she and the families walked in. The executive staff were seated on the dais behind the podium. All the Mars station staff save two, were allowed to attend the service. Barton and Parker were the two to stay behind. For some reason I was not surprised at that. It was 0900 hours. Tanner took the stage.

"Call to Arms!" Tanner said with authority.

Everyone stood. The color guard responded by marching towards the podium. There were 4 people with guidons and two each turned in opposite directions, on either side of the podium. They stopped at the flag stands. Tanner called out the next command, "Present, Arms!" The color guard saluted the podium and then placed the guidons in the stands. They took a step back, turned on their heels and faced the audience with a salute. All the military personnel saluted and held it until Tanner gave the command, "Order, Arms!" Everyone put their arms down, but remained standing until the color guard marched off and recovered to the front alcove outside the assembly chamber.

"Please be seated," Tanner said in a more relaxed manner. "It is with great honor that I am here to salute the victims of this terrible tragedy." She continued with much compassion and did a fine job. Everyone retired to the cantina for a reception. It was decided that only the families and minimal staff would be present for the burial. While I was chatting with my staff, I noticed a little old lady go up to Tanner and talk to her. Tanner's expression was of great surprise and shock. She looked over to me and called me over. "Doctor, this is Madam Miranda De Courvier. She is Louis Frechette's mother!"

"Mother? How can that be?"

The elderly lady spoke clearly. "I believe I can explain. My dear Louis was born into a very poor home. We could not afford to send him to school so my mistress, my employer showed great kindness by legally adopting him. Unfortunately, she died in a horrible car crash and Louis was badly injured. He was in a coma for 2 years. We had given up hope and decided to end his life support service. By some miracle he survived but lost part of his memory. He never recovered all of it but some. He had entered GASA service and didn't really know much about his own past."

"Madam, forgive me. If I had known-"

"It's quite all right Doctor. I was able to establish a relationship with Louis years ago. I guess he just never got around to updating his records."

Tanner interjected. "There is still time to make arrangements for his remains. Madam, do you have a request?"

"Louis, loved space and everything connected with it. He wanted to explore but he was a little older than his peers. It took a lot for GASA to accept him. I believe a burial in space would have been his choice."

"It would be our honor."

Chapter 14

MISSION TO ALPHA CENTAURI B

September 20, 2169 1100 Hours

Captain Tanner gave the crew the day off after the funeral. We had finally received orders to leave Mars orbit and explore the rest of the Solar System. I spent some time with Madam De Courvier and then after lunch I saw her off back to Earth and decided to call Bill.

"Hey Sweetie!" He was excited to see it was me. "How are things on Mars?"

"Busy, but finished, thankfully. How is the exciting world of law?"

"It's been quiet. Boring, really. I've been spending a lot of time with your parents."

"Oh?" I was glad they were getting along. "What embarrassing things have they been telling you?"

"Oh not much." They talked more about your cousin, Darius."

"Really?"

"Yeah they really seem to get you two mixed up. Your mom, especially."

"We spent a lot of time together as kids."

"Your Dad pulled me aside and told me your mom just finished her Alzheimer's treatments so to take what she says with a grain of salt."

"That makes sense. Sometimes there are some lingering effects."

"That's only in rare cases, right?"

"Yes." I felt Bill was probing for more information but I shrugged it off. I was going to tell him how I felt, especially after the Mars incident and Barton's unique gender transition. "Bill, I miss you."

"I miss you, too."

"I think I will come back after this tour of duty."

"Are you saying what I think you're saying?" He sat up with anticipation.

"Yes. I will marry you when I get back."

"Awesome!" Bill jumped up and ran around the room. "I'll start the wedding preparations! Should we set a date?"

"Not yet. Let's wait until most of my tour is done."

"You have made me the happiest man in the solar system!"

"I need you to do one thing, though."

"Name it."

"Let me tell my parents. I want them to know before we leave Mars orbit."

"No problem. Make it fast though. I'm supposed to have dinner with them tonight."

"Will do. I love you."

"I love you, too, Sweetheart."

"Talk to you at dinner."

"See you then." The com screen went dark. I took a deep breath and dialed my parents. I didn't feel scared but I was a little nervous. My Dad answered. "Hi Sweetie! How are you?"

"I'm fine, Dad. Is Mom with you? I have some exciting news."

"Yes she's in the kitchen. Hold on." Dad stood up and called to the kitchen, "Hey Dot! Endana is on the com!" My mother came in immediately. "Hi Danna! How are you, Honey?"

"I'm great, Mom. I have some important news. Bill and I are getting married."

All the color dropped out of their faces. Dad spoke first, "Really? Wow. I mean congratulations!"

Mom composed herself and spoke, "That's great! And he knows about the change?"

"No, Mom. I haven't told him."

"I see. Are you?"

"I wasn't planning on it. I didn't see the need."

"Well, that's something to consider. If you tell him right away, he has time to adjust. Dropping something like that as you as walking down the aisle is not the best way to start a life together."

"I understand. I have time."

Dad chimed in. "So are you coming home, now?"

"No. I will finish this tour of duty and then come home."

"Will you leave GASA? I mean you've worked so hard for a long time."

"Not sure, yet. I would like to stay in, maybe work on base in a clinic. I enjoy doing research so maybe I can do that. I'll know better after we have been in space for a while."

"That's sounds great. But I share your mother's concern about telling Bill the truth. We can't really advise you about what the right thing to do is but this is a big step. At least consider it."

"I will, Dad. I love you guys. I need to finish up some things but I will call you at dinner. We are set to leave orbit at 1900 hours so I will call you an hour before."

"Okay, kiddo. Love you."

"Love you, too."

I really never thought I'd have to tell Bill I used to be a man. It seemed so long ago but it's only been a few months. I contemplated the pros and cons of telling him. Somehow, I didn't think it would be catastrophic. He was the first man to know me as only a woman; all my friends and extended family think I am somewhere else as a man. I know that GASA made up an 'official' story but I now realize I never actually read it. I thought about it during lunch and figured I should check it out. I walked back to my quarters and sat down at my com. I typed in my name (I could have just spoken into the com but I was concerned about prying ears) and waited. Download time was slower since we were preparing to leave orbit. Once the data came through, I transferred it to my pad and laid down on my bed. After sifting through the usual standard documents, I came across this one:

GLOBAL AIR AND SPACE AGENCY
Combined Systems Command
Medical Division
3630 Stanley Rd #12501
San Antonio, TX 78234

REPORT AS OF 15 JULY 2169

PROFILE: Darius Obama
RANK: Lieutenant Commander
MOS: Doctor of Medicine
CURRENT DUTY POSITION: Chief Medical Officer, USS Kennedy
STATUS: Indefinite Convalescent Quarantine

Lieutenant Commander Darius Obama was a member of the landing team that encountered the Venus Anomaly that affected the USS Kennedy and required a quarantine of the entire ship and crew. The anomaly caused a catastrophic genetic breakdown of all affected crew members. Once the anomaly was contained, the USS Kennedy was delivered to Mars for a full decon and reconstitution.

(A decon and reconstitution means that the whole ship was scrubbed clean and renovated, with a new crew. It's like an overhaul. Ships that can't be reconstituted are scuttled and sent to the scrap yard on the dark side of the moon.)

The affected crew members, including LC Obama were sent to the GASA Extended Convalescent Center, Melbourne, Australia where they remain as of the date of this report.

MEDICAL EVALUATION

It is with great importance and sadness that the judgement of this command has decided that the affected crew members of the USS Kennedy will remain at the Convalescent Center for the rest of their lives, with full benefits and pay. This decision does not come lightly nor easily. The tragic circumstances in which these people were injured are unlike anything any human being has experienced. It is because of the tremendous amount of risk that comes with space exploration we deem that these men and women will be cared for until they depart this life. This decision was made using the most advanced medical technology, the most exhaustive testing available, relative documentation and all available data applicable to such a unique situation.

The final point of this report is that the afflicted crew members must remain cloistered due to the possible contagious nature of their sickness. For the public good, the crew members have agreed to relinquishing any and all contact with the outside world, in exchange for compensation for their families and loved ones.

These men and women are held in the highest esteem by GASA and the world aeronautical/space community. May God have mercy on their lives and souls.

> *Michael Sennett*
> *LTC, USA*
> *AMEDD Commander*

I was more shocked than I thought I would be; the report contained far more compassion from the Medical Command than I expected. I had hoped they were thorough enough to erase our entire digital footprint. This would be extremely hard to explain if anyone suspected any kind of cover up.

I found myself somewhat tired after reading the report and some of the 'data' the Medical Command used to put our male selves into exile. It was quite good. I was glad that it convincing enough to satisfy prying eyes. I put down my pad and dozed for a while. My mind seemed to wander, to Bill, my folks and then it landed on a thought. Someone knows the truth. I sat straight up. "Cleveland!" My brain was yelling. I had to figure out what angle his was. Maybe Bill can help. I bounded off my bed and fired up my com.
"What's up? I thought you were going to call at dinner."
"Sorry-I still will but I need a favor."
Bill smiled. He liked when I asked him for a favor. "What can I do for you, Doctor?"
"Do you remember that guy we met last month, Cleveland?"
"Yeah, Mister Snoopypuss. Is he bothering you again?"
"No, but I need to find out about him. He pulling some shenanigans and it involves classified information."
Bill got serious. "Wow, that's serious business. You want me to vet him?"

"Yes. I need everything you can find out about him. Childhood, school records, the works."

"I will get right on it. It's a slow day here in the office anyway."

"Thanks, Hun. Talk to you at dinner."

"Look forward to it."

I thought of Wilson and how we'd agreed to deal with Cleveland after the Mars incident was settled. I called her and brought her up to speed.

"So when will you hear?"

"Any time now. He's working on it as we speak."

"What do you think Cleveland wants?"

"Well here's my theory-since he knows what happened on the Venus Mission, he's trying to find a way to cash in."

"How could he have found out?"

"Well let's go with the obvious. He is (or was) a member of GASA. He already knew about us when he contacted us. He has some information but not all of it. He is patient. He has contacts."

Wilson pondered for a moment. "If he wants to cash in, he is planning something big. He needs the complete story, plus the related data."

"Right. I think that about covers it. Hopefully, Bill can fill in the larger gaps."

"I can't imagine what Cleveland hopes to achieve."

"Let's hope it's something less sinister than he is leading us to believe."

Wilson nodded and went to her quarters. I decided to go to the Viewing Deck. It was only the second time I visited there. Sometimes we get so busy that we forget the beauty of the stars. I peered into the black void looking at the Martian sky. I wondered if I would be happier on Earth with a husband and a family. I think I could be, but there was something out in that black void. Something to discover, to see, to understand. The Anti-space sentiment crossed my mind. Were they right? Is it our place as human beings to go beyond our planet, our solar system? I have always believed in God, the Judeo-Christian version. People have questioned His existence for eons and now there is a real possibility of meeting Him without crossing into the Great Beyond permanently, I hope. I continued my philosophical musings as I sat in the comfortable lounge chair. The door slid open behind me and it was Tracy and Tanner.

"Ladies. How are you?" I liked having the company. It was perfect timing.

"We're ready to get out of Dodge." Tanner was noticeably excited.

"Me too. Mars is depressing. I'm ready to see the rest of the solar system." I hadn't seen Tracy in days. I turned to her. "What have you been doing? I haven't seen you."

"Just tweaking the engines. We're going to be doing light speed a lot more often."

"Will we need light speed for a while? I figured we wouldn't use it until we got beyond Pluto."

"Do you want to tell her?" Tracy said to Tanner.

Tanner smiled. "We have new orders. Due to the positive additional testing on Mars, GASA has approved us for deep space."

"Okay, so that mean we-" Tracy interrupted me. "We are skipping our solar system! We headed towards Alpha Centauri B!"

"That's incredible! Are we going to be able to study the Theorites?" (The Theorites are the nickname for planets that were assumed to exist in the Alpha Centauri B galaxy that would most likely be able to support life

"Not only that, if conditions are favorable, we'll be the first ship to evaluate them for colonization!"

"Holy crap! That will make history! Wow. I can't believe it! We'll be the first humans on an alien world! Outside our solar system I mean." I was excited. "Imagine all the research we can do!"

"We'll be there in four days at double light speed. We'll need to work out a game plan for the landing party and obviously I want you there."

"Didi, we should not rush to the surface. We should do as much long range scanning as possible."

"Why so cautious?"

"Well since the Venus Mission we're facing things no human has ever dealt with. I don't want to end up an alien reptile man or something." Didi and Tracy looked at me. They knew I was serious, but they looked at each other and burst out laughing. I laughed too. Didi wiped her eyes. "Okay, Doc. We will be extra careful."

We left the Viewing Deck and headed down for dinner. "I will catch up with you guys. I need to make a phone call first."

"Don't be long, I ordered Prime Rib to celebrate going to Alpha Centauri." Didi smiled. She had been waiting for this for a long time.

I was excited to tell my family about the new mission. I almost forgot that I wanted to talk to Bill alone first. I called him and it took a little longer to go through. He was walking up to my parent's house when he answered. He answered through his pad, which would account for the slower connection. "Hey Sweetheart."

"Hi Sweetie." He looked serious.

"What did you find out?"

"Well, it took some really effort. I called in a few favors and got probably more than I was supposed to."

"Do tell."

"First, Philip Ivan Cleveland is dead, and has been for forty years. He was the only Phillip Cleveland to serve in GASA."

"You have to be kidding me."

"No. The Philip Cleveland you know is a security specialist named Romulus Rood. He is part of the United Nations Global Security force on loan to GASA for deep space security operations."

"'Deep Space Security Operations? We need that?"

"Apparently, the UN thinks we do."

"Interesting. Anything else?"

"Yes. He has a wide scope to do what he thinks is necessary."

"Wow. You called in some serious favors."

"Actually, it's because of you."

"What do you mean?"

"When I kept getting stonewalled through normal channels, I contacted your special friend, Governor Stevens. He is on the National Deep Space Security Committee, special liaison to the UN."

"That's uncanny luck."

"Gift horse in the mouth and such. Anyway, most the information is from him and he is willing to keep us abreast of developments in that area."

"So why is Cleveland, Rood, after classified information?"

"That we do not know. It's possible he wants to know for security reasons."

"I wish. He contacted another of my crewmates and lied about who is wife was."

"He's a spy. It doesn't surprise me."

Bill paused for a moment. He seemed nervous.

"What's the matter, Sweetie?"

"Governor Stevens was more than generous in sharing information.

Even highly classified information. In the process of getting all this information, I read about the Venus Mission."

Not much has shaken me since my gender change. I haven't felt nervous or scared, until Bill said those words.. "What did you find out?"

"Everything." I started to tear up. "Did you read it carefully? I mean from beginning to end?"

"Yes. I know everything. I know that you are, were Darius Obama. I know that you risked your life to help your crew mates and that you found out too late that you could not change back to male, even if you wanted to."

"I didn't want to lie to you, Bill, I just didn't know how to tell you."

"It's okay. I also read the medical data and saw that you aren't just transgender, you have been completely changed over to female. Your reproductive organs, genes, everything."

"What are you saying?"

Bill relaxed and smiled. "I'm saying that I would have been awfully bummed out if we couldn't have children!"

Months of tension that I had forgotten about ran out of my body. If had not been an enhanced female, I probably would have developed ulcers over it. "Oh Bill, you mean you still want me?"

"Of course! I've only really gotten to know you as Endana. I guess I will miss Darius but we only saw each other summers on the Cape anyway. You are now the woman I love and that all I know you as. My feelings have not changed. Just make sure you come back to me so we can start a family."

"I will! I love you so much!"

"I love you too. Let's tell your folks."

Chapter 15

LIGHTSPEED

September 20, 2169 1800 Hours

The crew met in the cantina. With a skeleton team on the bridge monitoring the last of the mission prep, Tanner called the meal to order. "I have called everyone here as well as simulcasting this to the bridge. I am proud and pleased to announce our new mission. We are headed to the Alpha Centauri B galaxy to not just explore but colonize a planet!"
The crowd went wild. Tanner ordered Champagne and it went from dinner to a party. We ate and drank for a while. We laughed and congratulated each other and talked about what we were going to do on the first planet we found. Everything from building a mineral spa to an aerogel drone farm and more were dreamed up. The excitement of the night lasted for hours. I left for a little while and glammed up my look. Tanner, Tracy and several others followed suit and we partied for several hours.   About midnight, things subsided and Tanner went to the bridge to initiate leaving orbit. We all returned to our duty stations for this event all though most of us were off duty. I accompanied Tanner to the bridge. She sat in her command chair and prepared to give the order to leave orbit. We turned on the ship-wide com so everyone could hear the command. I sat on the bridge at the

medical console and turned forward. Tanner savored the moment.
She turned and looked at all of us, one by one. She knew we were
proud to serve under her and she, us.
Tanner sounded the Bosun's Call.
"All hands, this is Captain Tanner. We are about to embark on the
greatest mission, no-the greatest adventure mankind has ever faced.
We will experience things no human being has ever seen and maybe
never again. Let me urge you to document your daily lives, your
work, your recreation and your emotions as we travel into the
Greatest Unknown. May God have mercy on us and may we return
with a greater understanding of ourselves and of our very existence.
Our goal is to travel to the Alpha Centauri B galaxy and find a planet
to colonize. We will be conducting many smaller missions, mostly
research and scientific but we have the unique opportunity to see
another part of the universe that no other human has ever seen. And
now I'd like to give you a statement based on an introduction from a
centuries old television show about this very experience:

*Space. The last frontier. This is the second voyage of the
United Star Ship Kennedy. Our mission: to travel beyond our solar
system. Our goal: to explore new worlds and seek out new life, to
preserve our own culture and discover the unknown. We hope that in
the event that we meet alien life, we can not only communicate but
establish common grounds and friendship. We travel into the depths
of space and seek understanding of ourselves as well as the
unknowable.*

Godspeed, my friends. Take us out of orbit, Mr. Christian."

"Aye, sir." The navigator brought the ship out of orbit. We were still
moving albeit slowly. We all held our breath. Tanner spoke calmly.
"Set course for the Alpha Centauri system."
"Course laid in and set."
"Light speed one. Engage."
As we watched the main screen it was like a movie. The stars and
planets stretched and caught up with themselves. We felt a slight
amount of inertia as the Kennedy jumped to lightspeed. "FTL-1,
Light speed achieved, Sir."

"Maintain course. Steady as she goes."

"Aye."

I spoke first. "Congratulations, Commander."

"Thank you, Doctor."

I checked the console screen and everything was normal. It was then that I realized that myself and the Captain were still in party dress. I stood up and moved over to the command chair. "Are you going to change?"

"Not yet," Tanner was still staring at the view screen. "I still feel somewhat, celebratory."

I stood there for a few minutes, experiencing what no one has ever achieved before, marveling at the fact we were traveling beyond our own solar system. We had achieved full light speed within our solar system for testing and short expeditions but never has anyone gone beyond Saturn. As amazing event as this was I decided to go to bed and be fresh for the next day. "I'm going to turn in."

"I'm going to stay up a little while longer." Tanner was transfixed.

"Good night, Didi."

Tanner finally broke her gaze from the view screen and turned to me. "Good night, Danna, and thanks."

"For what?"

"For being part of this."

I nodded and smiled. Didi did the same and turned back to the view screen. "Ensign, enhance magnification. I want to see more."

September 21, 2169 0700 Hours

I woke up more refreshed than I expected. I was excited because we were headed toward deep space. I wondered what we would find in the Alpha Centauri System. I wondered what was there if we found any of the Theorites. I called Tanner on the com. "Morning Captain."

"Morning, Doc."

"Have you been to bed?"

"I tried. Took an hour nap but I was too excited."

"Well, tonight you should turn in early. You can't explore space half asleep."

"Yes, Doctor." She smiled a wry grin.

"You hungry?"

"Yes, actually. Breakfast?"

"Twenty Minutes."

"Done." The com screen went dark and I got dressed. I decided on a slightly pronounced look for the day. Not sure why but didn't give it too much thought. I went to sickbay to check the day's tasks. No one was sick so I decided to look into the Eleusian drive analyses progress. It had been several weeks since I worked on it so I recapped a little. We still needed to know why the Mars archive upload caused the Mars explosion. Since the funeral service for the victims, GASA has given us a lot of room to deal with it. They were concerned about bad publicity and raising the ire of the Anti-space advocates. They can be more than a nuisance (especially when it comes to funding) so GASA treads carefully. The science lab team made significant progress during my absence. I spoke with Tracy and she said Jamie Braddock had made some significant discoveries. I had only seen Jamie in passing in the past few weeks. She had immersed herself into the Eleusian Data and was now the foremost expert. She looked a little tired but she was in good spirits. She was an attractive girl. Sometime after her gender change she had changed her hair color. She was a light brown brunette, but now she was a platinum blonde.

"Nice hair color."

"Hey Doc. It's been a while. Yeah I'd forgotten that we hadn't seen each other for a while. I got using to being a blonde."

"It looks good on you. What's the latest on the drives?"

"You wouldn't believe it. We've found cures to all sorts of diseases. Did you know that chicken pox was a weapon? The Eleusians didn't realize that over time we would build up a resistance to it. By the 20th century, it was a mild nuisance. Children could overcome it with a little care. I guess they expected the children to carry it a lot longer so it would sterilize them as adults but it was a failure. Cancer could have been eradicated 130 years earlier if we had this data."

"That's amazing. Too bad we didn't get to Venus sooner."

"That's only the surface. There are exabytes of data that had the Eleusians ruling the Earth for thousands of years. If they hadn't fought among themselves, they'd probably still be around. Also, we would have traveling the stars hundreds of years ago."

"All that time wasted. Just because of foolish pride."

"Do you know what the real tragedy is?"

"Do tell."

"This gender change thing? You'll never guess why it was created."

"Why? Is it another weapon?"

"Not at all. It started off as a super soldier program. Their females were far more durable physically than the males. The males were the equivalent of our best male specimen; the females were better. They literally dismantled their own female genome and reengineered it. Then they tried to enhance their natural born females, but they rejected it. They could not rewrite the original female genetic code. So a small group of male Eleusian scientists tried it on themselves and were successful. Too successful."

I was fascinated. "Let me guess. It got away from them."

"Well, in a sense. They did end up turning themselves into enhanced females like us. Once that happened, they viewed it as a gift. But something else happened. They accidentally created a super-virus that carried the genetic formula to change male to female. They also created the cure. But as we already know, it has to be administered within thirty days or they became female permanently."

"Fascinating."

"Would you like to hear the kicker?"

"Absolutely."

"It was a prank."

"I'm sorry, what?"

"The final administration of the virus was a prank. Ares was Aphrodite's lover but Zeus was jealous. For some weird reason, Ares wanted to mess with Zeus and tried to turn his armies into women. Zeus thought women were still inferior for some reason. Ares thought the female soldiers would embarrass Zeus when they met the men on the battlefield. Ares was correct and Zeus was furious. The problem, however, is that Ares never told Zeus he could change the women back into men. The pheromone levels were so high that the enhanced women's libidos were completely out of control and not only that," I interrupted Jaime because I knew what was next. I continued her sentence. "The men began change into women spontaneously."

"Yes! How did you know?"

"Because it can still happen. I've done it."

"What?"

"CPO Barton. On Mars. He turned into a woman when I flirted with him really hard."

Jaime was shocked. "You did that?"

"I pretty sure that I did. I didn't mean to. I mean he was gay and I was wondering how my pheromones would affect him, if they did at all!"

"So he was gay, and you flirted with him? Why?"

"It was an informal experiment. I knew that we had the heightened pheromone production, but I never thought it would turn him into a woman."

"You flirted with him and then what happened? How did he react?"

"He was flustered for sure. He had a partner, so he was somewhat confused. I backed off and I felt really bad I messed with him."

"Did you feel any changes when you did that?"

"I felt a little warm, I mean not like amorous, just a slight rise in body temperature."

"I never guessed that was something we could control. I'll need to run some tests."

"We need to keep this under our hat; only you, me and Tanner know. Barton has no idea about the Venus mission or anything."

"Okay."

Just then Cleveland crossed my mind. "Jaime, what did you do on furlough last month?"

"I went home to London. I told my mother about the change. It took a few weeks for her to deal with it. My dad died last year so I am all she has. She's okay now."

"That's good. Did you have anyone visit you unexpectedly? From GASA?

"Come to think of it, there was a guy who contacted me. His name was Cleveland, I think."

"What did he want?"

"He wanted to talk about the Venus Mission and what happened. I didn't end up meeting with him though. We talked briefly over comms and I claimed I couldn't discuss it with him. My mom was having a hard enough time as it was."

"Did he have a wife with him?"

"I don't know. He called me from his office. He didn't mention his wife."

"Okay. If you remember anything about him, let me know. It's very important."

"Will do. I have a lot more to tell you about the drives so we'll meet later?"

"Sure."

Captain Cleveland is very persistent. I thought I should ask the same question of the commander. I went up to meet her for breakfast. She was already at the cantina studying her pad over fruit and some tea. I sat down. "I have to tell you something."

"We have much to talk about. You first."

"Did a Captain Cleveland contact you during your furlough?"

"Yes. Why?"

"He's contacted a bunch of us. His name isn't Cleveland either. It's Romulus Rood."

"He told me he was with JAG office."

"He's a spy. He knows what happened on the Venus Mission and he's been pumping a lot of us to get more information."

"Interesting. He seemed very interested about biological data. He knew we found something on Venus but he didn't seem to know exactly what."

"I got the same vibe. Any ideas on what we should do?"

"Well he can't get to us out here. I'd put it on the back burner until we get back. Maybe he'll lose interest."

"I don't think he will. Not since he's gone to great lengths to find us."

"Still, unless he stowed away on this ship, he can't get to us."

"True. I guess I can forget about him for now."

"Seeing we are on our way to another galaxy, I think that's a great idea." Didi smiled.

"So, moving on to other things I just had an enlightening conversation with Lieutenant Commander Braddock."

"She's been tireless on the drives. I almost had to order her to take some time off."

"Well it hasn't been for naught. She has some vital information about the drive data."

Didi shifted in her seat. "Give me the Reader's Digest version."

It seems that the gender changing serum was a prank gone wrong."

"You have to be joking!"

"I wish I was. Such a crime for all of that technology lost to the human race because supposedly superior beings were acting like immature children."

"Can you imagine?"

"Braddock says we would have been out here 175 years earlier, if the Eleusians kept their crap together."

"That makes me kind of pissed. We could have done so much more with their discoveries. Avoided war, poverty, disease, it's the ultimate diss."

"Well there's more." I proceeded to tell Didi everything. About the flirting with Barton, the subsequent gender change and the pheromones. She was amazed. "We are extremely lucky Barton wanted to transition. You could have had a catastrophe on your hands."

"That's true. I just felt bad that I had messed with him. If I had any idea that this would have happened, I never would have tried it."

"We are in a unique position. I guess it will take some time to fully understand our condition. For now, keep this under wraps. We don't want any more informal experiments. Plus, the men on the ship won't have a snowball's chance if we let this slip. Even I'm struggling not having my man around me."

"The pheromone balance vapor should be sufficient to keep everyone on an even keel. I have an alarm set if the pheromone balance starts to tip."

"Okay that's good. Let's move on to landing party protocols."

September 21, 2169 1430 Hours

The morning had been productive. We worked out landing party protocols and now they were circulating through the ship's sections for edits, acknowledgements and suggestions. I grabbed a late lunch and headed up to the bridge. I'll be spending more time there as we travel towards Alpha Centauri. As Chief Medical Officer, there wouldn't be much to do until we got to the first planet. Ensign Thornton, bruised his shoulder playing racquetball and there was a minor Gallium gas leak in the fiber optic array; otherwise sickbay was relatively quiet. I spent more time in the science lab with Braddock learning about the Eleusians and their technology. We decided to synthesize as many cures for diseases still active on Earth in order to bring them back. We can say we developed them in the process of colonization and new gather data from another planet. That would ensure that no one would connect the data to the Venus Mission, keeping our secret.

I called Bill once I was done with my duty day and we chatted. He had no more information about our friend Cleveland and I didn't press him. "How's Mom and Dad?"

"They're great. Your Mom has adopted me and your Dad has had me golfing 3 times already. To be honest with you, I've met some interesting people on the golf course. I may even open my own practice."

"Really? You never mentioned that before."

"I never really gave it any thought until recently."

"Are you going to do it?"

"Not right now. I may give it some thought after you get back."

"Okay."

Bill paused for a long time. "What is it?"

"I guess I never thought about a private practice. It's a risk."

"Well stick with the firm until I come home. Then I can get a job as a doctor somewhere and you can get your practice started."

"You're okay with that? I mean you'd leave the service for me?"

"Let's save that answer for when I'm coming back. I might have had enough of the service when I'm done."

"I love you."

"Love you, too."

"One more thing: It may be tough to make these calls once we leave the solar system. They may have to be recorded and sent subspace."

"I understand. I'll have to call you a lot more often until then."

"You'd better."

Bill smiled and the screen went dark. I really hadn't given a lot of thought to my post mission plans. I thought I would spend a lot more time in GASA but now I wasn't sure. I decided to put off those thoughts until I could act on them, one way or another. Before I got up, Tanner called and asked me to come up to the bridge. "You'll want to see this."

"On my way." I moved quickly to the bridge and moved towards the medical console. Tanner motioned me to the command chair.

"Doctor, I present to you, the Alpha Centauri system." She gestured toward the view screen. I saw a myriad of unfamiliar constellations, gas clouds that splashed a thousand colors. "It's beautiful."

"Breathtaking. Not only that in less than an hour of long range scanning, we've found three theorite planets with an almost sustainable atmosphere. Colonization will be a lot easier than we thought!"

"Incredible! I never thought it would be this fast."

"The first planet is one we've been able to learn a lot about from Earth over the last 200 years, known as Alpha Centauri B. It's relatively identical to Earth with a 15 month orbit around the sun, slightly cooler global temperatures and possibly an atmosphere."

"Could it have an ecosystem?"

"Scientists have theorized that there is a 87 percent chance of some type of vegetation and animal life on the planet with a temperate climate in the higher latitudes and warmer towards the planet's' Equator. I have to believe that it's too much to hope for intelligent life."

"At this point anything is possible. How long until we achieve an orbit?"

"About 48 hours. We started scanning about four hours ago and we have only received atmospheric data so far. Nothing about the surface, yet."

"I will keep an eye on the scanning. I want to know what we're going to face on the surface."

"Okay Doc."

I left to check my console and the headed to the science lab. I hadn't spoken to Jamie for a while. We would need to be prepared to shuttle down the surface of Alpha Centauri B. I was excited to think about what we would find. I entered the lab and found Jamie working on a pressure suit. We use them to do space walks, exterior ship maintenance (a rare occurrence) and they are designed for surface exploration. The suits are equipped with comms, waste filtration system and propulsion. Jamie wanted to make them lighter but it was not a high priority. As enhanced females, we are 400% stronger than we were as men so the original weight of the suits was negligible. Still, Jamie wanted every advantage due to the risk of exploring a new world. They were impressive upgrades. "How goes it?"

"Great. Using the Eleusian data, I've been able to increase the jetpacks' output by 47 percent. I redesigned the under-suit and used micro-hydraulics to increase efficiency levels with the cooling systems and waste filtration. It's been a lot of fun!"

"I'm glad you're having a good time." I said that tongue in cheek but it really has been a blessing to have the Eleusian data to help us. I spent the rest of the day in the lab and then broke for dinner. I decided I'd take the next day off and relax. I'm sure there would be a lot of work to do when we got to Centauri B. Little did I know what an understatement that would be.

Chapter 16

THE ARRIVAL

September 22, 0947 Hours

I had a surprisingly restful day off. I didn't want to call home so I could just focus on the mission. I was on my way back to sick bay from breakfast when the Bosun's Call was sounded. Tanner's voice was clear over ship wide comms. "Ladies and Gentlemen. We have arrived in the Alpha Centauri system. As I will not announce every port of call we enter, this one is historic. We are the first human beings to make it this far out into space, the first humans to leave our galaxy and enter a new one. As we discover the fantastic, we are pretty much on our own. We will be traveling to the first planet that we suspect can support human life and explore it. From now on, the established exploration and landing protocols are in effect."
I decided to go to the bridge and get a full glimpse of the system. I entered the lift and Tracy was coming up from engineering.

"Pretty exciting, isn't it?"

"Sure is."

"Think we'll find anything on Centauri?

"Anything is possible. I just hope we are not disappointed." I'm not sure why I said that. I had no reason to think we'd be disappointed since we had no idea what we were facing. We stepped onto the bridge and took our respective seats. "Good morning, Doctor."

"Morning, Captain. How goes it?"

"Doctor, in ten minutes we will enter orbit around Centauri B. I am so nervous. In a good way."

"I feel the same way. Anything on long range?"

"Not sure yet. Centauri seems to have some debris in orbit. Probably space rock dust caught in the outer atmosphere."

"That's amazing."

"There's another scan report coming in in a few minutes. Lieutenant Harrison, do we have any new data."

"Not yet, Ma'am. Should be here in a few minutes."

"Okay, thank you. Doctor, can you scan for organic material, vegetation of any kind? Microbes and such."

"Aye, Captain." We smiled at each other as I moved over to my medical console. I entered the parameters and started scanning. We were minutes away from orbit so I stayed at the console. What I saw next was nothing short of historic. I watched the console screen and couldn't believe my eyes. The scan not only found vegetation, but life forms. Human life forms. I ran a full diagnostic and the scanned a second time. Then a third. After the tenth scan with the same results, I told the Captain. "Commander, you need to see this."

"What is it?" She walked over to my console and her jaw dropped. "Is this for real?"

"I scanned ten times adjusting the parameters and tweaking everything I could."

"There can't be people down there. Nobody has been out here."

"We need to go down there to investigate."

Tanner turned to the bridge crew. "Ms. Harrison, prepare an away team!" She turned to me and smiled with excitement. "I have been waiting all my life to say that!" We both smiled. I got up and pulled my landing pack from under the console. Tanner grabbed her landing pack and we moved toward the lift. "Harrison, you have the bridge.

Keep scanning the planet and stay in radio contact."

"Aye, Captain. Be careful."

Tanner nodded and smiled. We met the rest of the party in the shuttle bay. Tanner asked me to give a quick briefing before we departed. There were eight crew members on the team. I was a little nervous. "Long range scanners have detected an atmosphere and organic, human life. We have no idea what we're walking into so standard protocols are in place until further notice. The most important thing is to stay in groups, pairs at a bare minimum and only if absolutely necessary. We will lose no one, is that understood?" The group responded and we boarded the shuttle. I punched in the coordinates of the scanning reference point, which would have been the last location of the life form we detected. Jennings, a young ensign from xeno-biology seemed on edge. "Doctor, how is it possible that there's human life here?"

"I honestly don't know, Ensign. That's what we're going to find out."

"Is there any possibility of someone making it out here this far? I thought we were the first."

"As far as I know we are. I mean there were urban legends of the earlier GASA missions sending probes and ships out here but officially nothing manned."

"You're talking about the Argos missions?"

"Yes. As far as we know it was totally automated. No humans were sent beyond Mars. It was deemed too dangerous."

"My father was a mission control specialist with GASA 40 years ago. He was never able to confirm it but he said GASA used to do suicide missions. People with nothing to lose, terminally ill, the lost and forgotten were asked to do those types of missions. They were to send back as much information as they could." His voice trailed off. He seemed sad about it. "Don't worry Ensign, I'm sure that those are just old wives' tales. They get more fantastic as time goes on. We'll find out the truth soon enough."

The shuttle trip was only a few minutes but as we descended below the cloud we were astonished. We saw lush vegetation and a grand wide river. It was incredible. As we were in awe of seeing a new planet, Harrison spoke to us over comms. "Commander, we have new information."

"We copy. What's the latest?"

"You aren't going to believe this but there are metal structures about

6 kilometers from your current position."

"Metal structures? What kind of metal?"

"It's actually a Titanium Tungsten alloy, and there's chromium."

"Chromium? No one's used chromium in 40 years! At least on earth. Is it possible that this is an earth vessel of some sort?"

"Too early to tell, Captain. We are still trying to isolate other material data."

"Send me the coordinates and keep me posted."

"Aye, sending the coordinates now."

We flew another couple of minutes until we saw several metal structures. I moved up into the co-pilot's seat next to Tanner. A thought occurred to me. "It's possible it's just old space junk that we lost in space. It could have floated through space and fell here."

"But if that's true, we would have still beaten it here. The junk would have to have spent a couple of hundred years in space to get here, or it would have to travel at sublight speeds."

"What about a wormhole? They were postulating them over a hundred years ago."

"I suppose but the odds of a wormhole stable enough to bring that much debris are beyond calculation. Most wormholes are extreme fleeting. Unpredictable, even now."

We found the metal structures. They were cylindrical and spaced out over about 100 yards. We found a clearing by the river and landed the shuttle. Everyone donned protective suits and we exited the shuttle. Tanner spoke first. "So make sure you orientate your GPS to the Kennedy and we'll use the river as a reference point. We will start with two teams. Maintain radio contact and turn on your emergency beacons. Tanner to Kennedy,"

Harrison responded, "Kennedy here."

"Ms. Harrison, are you receiving the away team's beacons?"

"Yes, Ma'am. We have everyone."

"Excellent. Okay folks. Turn on cameras and recorders and let's see what out there."

"Doctor, you and I are senior staff so I will take A team towards the south and you take B team to the east. Let us know if you cross the river. Way points set and we're off."

"Be careful, Commander."

"You too, Doctor."

Chapter 17

A GALACTIC SURPRISE

We exited the shuttle and I did an atmospheric analysis.
"Commander, this air is breathable. It has slightly more nitrogen the Earth's but it's otherwise identical.
"Incredible, Doctor. Is it safe to take our breathers off?"
"As I would express extreme caution, it is. I would put them back on if the vegetation changes, plus everyone should keep their gas analyzers on."
"All right. Everyone can take off their breathers but have them ready." Tanner was flush with excitement. "Check in every 15 minutes."
As we moved towards the east we discovered a path. We saw that it was well worn, and we found footprints. I made an entry into my log as the camera panned across the path. We had confirmed that there was human or humanoid life here. The discovery just created more questions. Who were they? How did they get here? We continued down the path and came to a clearing. Beyond the clearing there was

a garden. We didn't recognize any of the fruit, but it was definitely cultivated by someone. The vegetables (I assumed they were) looked lush and delicious but I opted to leave it alone. I have memories of ancient movies where the space traveler ends up being eaten by a hungry plant. Something cheesy like that. I chuckled to myself and moved along with the others. I thought to take a sample of one of the plants but I waited. I wanted to find out what else was here in case something else was more significant.

We finally got to the first metal structure and I felt my jaw drop. I look up over the slanted doorway and saw the American Flag. Next to that was the name, USS Tempest. My team fanned out around the repurposed ship. While I was documenting this incredible find, I heard a voice behind me. "Who are you?"

Startled, I turned around fast and kept the camera facing in front of me. I saw a grey haired bearded man in his mid fifties. He was rugged, in good shape and dressed in some type of tattered uniform that was vaguely familiar. "I am Doctor Endana Obama, from the USS Kennedy. Who are you?"

"You wouldn't believe me if I told you."

"Right now, all bets are off on anything. Try me."

"I am Captain David Marteen, of the USS Tempest, or what left of it."

"You have to be kidding me. The Tempest was launched eighty years ago and lost."

"A suicide mission to say the least. It seems GASA has advanced enough to send you folks out here, or it was another one of Bradley's 'sacrifice for the future of man' missions. Come on into my home and I will explain." Marteen walked past me and into the hut. I contacted the Captain immediately. "You aren't going to believe this."

"I think I will. We will come to you."

I followed Marteen into the dwelling. It was on its side so the décor was surreal. There was century old technology repurposed for daily use. Some of the alterations were quite creative. "Coffee?" Marteen was very cordial.

"No, thank you."

"You must have many questions. Ask."

"How in the WORLD did you get here?"

Do you believe in God, Doctor?"

"Yes."

"I am a full believer. It was only by Divine Providence that we even survived that trip. When we landed a lot of us were banged up but we survived."

"How many of you are here?"

"Thirty. Well thirty original crew members. Once we realized we were marooned here, we pretty much became a community. A family. We have close to 100 people here now, including the children."

I was still trying to wrap my head around it. "The odds of you even making it out of the solar system were astronomical!"

Marteen flashed me a wry grin. I realized what I said, "No pun intended."

"Well, to be perfectly honest, we don't know. I was in command of the Tempest. See that bracket on the wall over there? That was my command chair. We started out from Earth. All of us either had some terminal disease or nothing to live for. I was supposed to be dead in two years or less. I was one of the better ones. Some had six months or less. Anyway, something hit us in space. We were able determine that it was an energy blast of some sort, based on the trajectory and direction, it could have come from this planet. It was an odd affect which seemed to put us into some kind of field, almost suspended animation. When we woke up, we were in the Alpha Centauri system and heading here. We could not change our course so we just held on for the ride. Once we entered the atmosphere, the ship began to spin, fast. Most of us were pinned to the walls and pretty shook up. We have no explanation as to what or who sent us here; what we do know is that if there was some type of intelligence, Supreme Being, God, whatever you choose to call it, it wanted us to survive."

"Captain Marteen, this is all well and good but you should be dead of old age. You are a middle aged man. It would have taken almost 300 years for you to get here with a ship like the Tempest. Even sub-light speed was theoretical when this ship launched."

"That's crazy! It's only been about 15 years since we've landed here."

"Captain Marteen,"

"David."

"David, today's Earth date is September 22, 2169."

Marteen was incredulous. "By our clocks, it's April 5, 2096."

"Let me show you." I took out my pad and pulled up ship's logs and the latest archival updates. Marteen took the pad and stared at it for a long time. "I can't believe it. How is this possible?"

I turned to CPO John Huang, Science Technician, assigned to our team. "What do you think, John?"

"If I had to guess, whatever pushed you out here did it at speeds it was not possible to achieve when you left Earth. "

I thought for a moment. "I agree, but even if they could, how could the Tempest have maintained hull integrity? Even at light speed, it would've been vaporized."

Huang mused. "Again, blame the energy blast. It may have created some kind of protective field around it. That's as plausible as anything else."

Marteen paced as he thought. "We had a ton of experimental technology on board when we left, anti-matter engines, xenon laser cannons and more."

John was curious. "Did you have any cobalt-beryllium diodes on board?"

"As a matter of fact we did. But we had discovered a significant flaw in the core. The uranium bands were degrading 6 times faster than the GASA scientists theorized. By the time we figured it out, the core was going critical and we couldn't stop it." Marteen paused for a moment and then laughed.

I was surprised. "What's so funny?"

"We jettisoned the core in order to save our lives. A ship full of terminally ill, suicidal people. How ridiculous!" I could see the dark humor Marteen was talking about. "Still, something happened that brought you here."

"Damned if we know. We tried figuring that out for a long time. Even after we landed here." Marteen moved over the oblong window the was once the ship's viewscreen.

I had a gnawing feeling in my gut. Their presence here made me ponder and I figured it had something to do with Eleusian technology. I snapped out of my daze. "We may have some resources on the Kennedy that could shed some light on this situation." Just then a group of three people come in. An attractive woman with two preteen children, a boy and a girl, dressed what I would call tribal clothing entered and looked at us. For obvious reasons, they were surprised to find us there. The woman walked over and kissed Marteen. "Darling, meet Dr. Obama, of USS Kennedy."

She got excited. "Are they here to rescue us? They've finally found us!"

"Not quite, but, sorry, forgive my manners. Doctor, this is my wife, Lieutenant Commander Barbara Baskin. She was my first officer."

"That's a new level of loyalty."

"We barely knew each other when we were assigned to the Tempest. She was a breast cancer patient. She had a double mastectomy but it was too late. They said she had about 8 months to live when we launched. We seemed to work well together then we got to be friends then when we got here we just stayed together until nature took its course. These are my children, Mark and Amanda."

"It's nice to meet you."

"We will meet the rest of the Community in a few hours. We typically have our meals together."

"Interesting. I would like very much to meet them. Captain Marteen, I do have a request."

"What is it?"

"I like to examine some of your crew members. It's seems you've outlasted your illnesses, and I'd like to know why."

"That's reasonable. They will have to give you their permission, though. We are somewhat of a democracy, here. We help each other but everyone pulls their weight. Even the children."

"Fair enough. Maybe we can give tours of the Kennedy."

The children's face lit up. Marteen smiled a father's smile. "We would like that, and if what you say is true, my people will have a lot of questions."

"I will make the arrangements. Let me contact my commander."

I stepped outside and called Tanner. I told her about what we found and the conversation I had with Marteen. I also mentioned that I believe much that has happened to these survivors has something to do with the Eleusians. "I will need to check the drives to find out for sure."

Tanner agreed. "Absolutely. We've found survivors too and they said their leader was Marteen. We'll need to compares notes to figure out the next step."

"Roger that. We are going to have lunch with the survivors and then meet up."

"We'll be joining them for lunch, too. See you then."

The next few hours were enlightening. Marteen showed us their garden, water purification, housing, systems and even games. They had a makeshift baseball field and other areas for recreation. Much of their lifestyle depended on repurposed materials from the Tempest. Fortunately, they had tools to develop natural available resources. Wood, sand for glass, and more. Once we had seen much of what they built, Marteen asked to speak to me privately. "I haven't told them this but we are in trouble."

"In what way?" I was curious to find out what could be wrong in such a Utopian setting.

"For a number of years, several of the original crew thought we could leave here. It took a great deal of effort to convince them otherwise, if at all. Now that you have arrived that is going to stir up emotions and desires to leave."

"You see that as a problem?"

"All of us were sick. That's why we were chosen for the mission to begin with. None of us expected to go back. We said our goodbyes and made peace with the finality of it all."

"Go on."

"As you have probably already figured out, this planet has given us a new lease on life. No one has been sick in a long time. Either we've been cured or there's something keeping us alive here."

"Have you tried to find out what it is?"

"Yes. For a long time after we outlived our illnesses, we wondered if it was temporary or permanent. We used all the salvaged equipment that we could find and make work but it wasn't enough. Anything we found was inconclusive. Hopefully, you can find out what it is."

"We'll do our best." I was confident that we could find the answer to this quandary.

Lunch time came and we met the rest of the Community. The Elders were the original bridge crew of the Tempest. They were considered more like advisors than leaders but their influence was pretty strong. The Community was peaceful and there didn't seem to be any animosity. We enjoyed very exotic fruits and vegetables. There was no meat offered due to the lack of any animals larger than a mouse. We talked with the children and the young adults.

It was somewhat idyllic existence yet they wanted more. They wanted to explore. Several of the original crew surveyed the land about 500 miles in each direction. They even built a bridge across the great river at its narrowest. Once we finished eating, I asked a couple of the original crew members if I could take blood samples and they were cooperative. I then asked some of the older teens and young adults and they cooperated as well. I secured the samples and got ready to return to the Kennedy. I found Marteen and spoke with him before I left.

"We are not in a hurry to leave. As a matter of fact the Captain is very interested in this planet and what happens here."

"I'm glad to hear that. If so much time has passed on Earth where things are not familiar anymore, some of us may stay."

"If that's the case, you won't be cut off. We'll make sure of that."

"Thank you, that means a lot."

Three Kennedy crewmen unloaded some communication equipment and supplies for Marteen and the Tempest Community. We shook hands as I got into the shuttle. We were airborne for a few minutes and I had a horrible thought. Our heightened pheromones! The Eleusian Effect! I had no idea if our enhanced pheromones had affected anyone on the planet. There was a much higher oxygen content in the atmosphere plus some unknown but harmless organic material. This will have to be considered. Research on the blood samples will take a while but we might be able to figure out this mystery. We had more questions than answers.

Chapter 18

MARCUS

September 22, 2169 1830 Hours

We joined Captain Tanner and discussed our unusual day over dinner. The whole bridge crew met and we told them about Marteen and his Community. One of the crewmen that was with Tanner had a strange expression on his face. I noticed it and asked. "Jack, what's the matter?"

"Nothing, Doctor, except-" he paused uncomfortably.

"What?"

"I overheard one of the children talk about someone named Marcus."

"Marcus?"

"Yes, it was very strange. They were saying things like, 'If we bring the newcomers to Marcus was, maybe it will give him back.' It was a little unnerving."

Tanner was amused. "Kids talking nonsense. Don't let it rattle you."

"They were pretty serious. They acted like it was some kind of monster."

"I'm sure it's probably their version of an old wives' tale but it would hurt to ask about it. Doctor, you seem to have a good rapport with Marteen. See what he has to say about it. Just to put it to bed."

"Will do. I will spend tomorrow analyzing those blood samples though, so I may not see him."

"Whenever it's convenient. Just to ease Jack's mind if nothing else." Tanner has a smirk on her face, but seemed genuine. Jack was still on edge but satisfied.

I decided to set up the blood tests after dinner but run them in the morning. I used the jacuzzi in the fitness center and retired for the evening. I wanted to be fresh for the morning so I avoided anything from the day's events. I caught up on some reading and made a video blog for Bill before I went to bed. I laid down and thought about Marteen and the mystery of his existence. There is so much in the cosmos that we haven't discovered yet and we're only just getting out here. What brought the Tempest out to this system? What healed the Tempest's crew and are they telling us everything? I hope to have some answers soon.

September 23, 2169 0700 Hours

I woke as refreshed as I hoped I'd be so I grabbed a quick breakfast and bolted down to the medical lab. Wilson met me and started analyzing the blood samples from the Tempest crew. We ran the standard tests first, then non-standard. Everything came out normal, meaning no signs of cancer or any other ailment. We ran a radiation test and used the method we used before, binding all the samples close to each other. We found a significant amount of an unknown radiation and with a deeper examination found trace elements of the unknown radioactive material. Jamie and Tracy came down at 0830 as I had asked them to, but I wanted first dibs on the samples. Jamie came first with Tracy trailing. "Whatcha' got, Doc?" Jamie looked at the scan first.

"Radiation. Unknown element."

"Effect?"

"Not sure. It seems to affect the mitochondria mostly but it has a steroidal effect at a cellular level."

"I've developed a data buffer with the Eleusian drives. Let me run it through."

"Okay, let me know what happens."

"Will do."

I decided to tell Tanner but just kept it between us until I could find out more. "So you think this mystery element is responsible for curing the Tempest crew?" Tanner was sipping tea.

"My personal opinion is yes, but scientifically it's too early to tell. We'll need to take soil samples from the planet and maybe even a deep subterranean scan."

"I will have the science department get on that."

"So, when do I get to chat with Captain Marteen? We didn't get a chance to talk earlier."

"Soon, I imagine. He's very interested in seeing the ship." Tanner pondered. "I'll have Yeoman Carruthers set up a ship's tour and a reception. They haven't seen any other humans for a long time so will need to handle them gently. Also let's limit their knowledge of the Eleusian issue. They shouldn't know anymore than our earth population about it."

"I agree. We are only about halfway through the data drive study as it is."

"Very good." I turned to leave when Tanner said, "Danna," They way she said it concerned me.

"Yes?"

"There's another issue that I need to talk to you about."

"Certainly. What is it?"

"You remember our friend, Captain Cleveland?"

"Unfortunately."

"It's seems he has friends in high places. I just received the first subspace comm packets and it has a rather sinister message."

"What does it say?"

"To make a long and uncomfortable session brief, once we have completed our current mission, we are to return to earth for an informational hearing."

"That doesn't sound so bad."

"At this hearing, we are to turn over all the Eleusian drives, related data any connected to it."

"That is not good."

"That's an understatement."

"Wait a minute! GASA promised us immunity and protection against any reprisal from dealing with the Eleusians! As far as the world know the crew of the Kennedy is sequestered in Australia for the rest of their lives."

"I know. This came from the White House. We have been assured that the hearing will be completely secure and private."

"Since Cleveland knows about what happened to us, I doubt very much that anything about these hearings will be private."

"I agree. We have almost a year to prepare. I'm open to any and all suggestions about how to deal with this."

"I will see what I can do. I have a friend that might be able to help."

"That's great. For now I will tell GASA that we will not address it until we return to Earth. Will a little fortitude, I think I can have them keep Cleveland at bay for now. We'll handle him when we get back."

I was relieved that Tanner could keep Cleveland out of our collective hair. But I was still furious. I stormed back to sickbay and tried to figure out the next move concerning Cleveland and the dog and pony show he was trying to create. After fuming for a couple of minutes, I decided to get my mind off of it by reviewing the results from the test of the unknown element (which, for brevity will now be referred to as Element X) we found in the Tempest crew's blood. What we found was definitely the reason they survived and also it was related to the Eleusians.

Chapter 19

OMNISPHERE

September 23, 2169 0912 Hours

Wilson, Tanner and myself (plus a normal away team) shuttled down to the planet to meet Marteen. We landed and brought supplies to Marteen's hut. I had a spare pad to give to Baskin to assist the Community. We met in common area to report the result of the test.
"Good Morning." Marteen and Baskin were finishing breakfast.
"Good Morning Doctor."
"Captain Marteen, you remember Captain Tanner."
"Yes we didn't get much chance to talk last time. Welcome."
"Thank you, Captain."
"David, please."

"Sure. I'll get right to the point. There is an unknown element here, we're calling it Element X, and we think it is responsible for your survival."

"Really? Is it a type of radiation?"

I was surprised. "How did you know?"

"As you remember, we made some discoveries but as I said we didn't have the equipment to learn much more."

I was impressed they had learned as much as that. I continued. "The radiation is caused by something on this planet. Each of you have trace amounts in your blood. It acts like a steroid but at the cellular level. It may also have slowed your aging, as well."

Marteen was thoughtful. "Is it a permanent condition? I mean if we leave here will it stop?"

"I am fairly confident that you are cured. The blood samples did not lose any radiation when we tested them. We'll monitor them for a few more days but the prognosis is promising."

Tanner spoke up. "Tell me David, have you guys been doing any kind of mining? I thought it an odd question but for some reason it made sense.

"Mining? No, but…" Marteen paused and a sad expression came over his face. I felt his sadness in that moment. "What is it?"

"There are caverns, a series of caves and valleys on the other side of the river, about 2 miles. We discovered them about eight years ago. We had considered making it another compound, but there was an accident."

"What happened?" Tanner asked with an equal amount of sadness.

"There was a particular area with extremely deep pits. They were pretty much bottomless-we couldn't see deep enough into them to know how far down they went. Our communications officer, Marcus Lockwood, was an amateur spelunker. He was from Colorado and often ventured into the Rockies to explore. He was terminal with colon cancer which is why he was on the Tempest. He was exploring near the pits and the ledge gave way. I told him he was too close and to back away but he ignored me. He seemed transfixed on the largest chasm. It was before we realized that we were cured. I guess he felt he had nothing to lose."

I remembered the story John Huang told about the children mentioning the name Marcus. "I'm sorry. That is tragic."

"We had a service for him but we never found his body."

Tanner spoke up. "I will have a shuttle fly over the chasm and scan it. Maybe we can find his body and give him a proper burial."

"Thank you, the community would like that." Tanner excused herself and made the call. I turned to Marteen, "To return to the original topic, we can start scanning for this unknown element as soon as the shuttle comes. We can do it while looking for Marcus."

"Sure, I'd like to be on that mission. I know the terrain and it will save some time."

I got the feeling that finding Marcus would give Marteen some closure. Tanner contacted the rest of the shuttle crew and coordinated with the ship's engineers to make sure we had the right equipment. We set launch time for two hours from now. We readied the shuttle with jet packs, winches and other recovery tools. Marteen opted for a jet pack and the engineers gave him a quick class on its operation. We launched the shuttle and Baskin guided us over to the caverns. Marteen, Baskin and three of our crew, Security Officer Jessica Barden (originally Bruce) and two engineers who were originally on the Venus Mission and changed by the virus, descended into the gaping, dark valley. Tanner and I were prepared to go down but Barden wanted to make sure the area was safe first. After an hour, Barden contacted us on the shuttle and gave the all clear. Tanner and I donned our jet packs and descended into the cavern. The shuttle landed in a nearby clearing. As I descended, I began to hear a low hum. "Captain, do you hear that?"

"Yes, I do. Fascinating."

We grew accustomed to it as we landed near the others. Luminescent plants gave the area a low light level. I decided to take advantage of it. "Lower your light and change them to red. It will be easier to use our natural night vision," I said to the others. The cavern floor was covered by a moss and it smelled like the moors. It was an earthy, smell like shallow swamps. We looked up and saw the sky through the narrow shaft we came down through. We began to explore. Tanner was on her guard. "Okay, everyone be extremely careful. We don't know what's down here. Captain Marteen, can you tell us anything about this cavern?"

"Not really. We've never been down here this far and after losing Marcus, the Elders deemed the caverns off limits."

"What about that noise?"

Marteen spun around. "What noise?"

"That low hum. Can't you hear it?"

"No, I don't hear anything."

"Saunders, Caspian, do you hear it?" They both confirmed it. Barden said she heard it too.

"How odd." Baskin said. "I don't hear anything either. Maybe it's because we've been here longer?"

"I suppose." I really didn't think that but I thought it best to move on and figure it out later. We trekked farther into the caves that were attached to the cavern. We left glowing markers to find our way out later. I took plant and soil samples as we moved deeper into the caves. When we stopped for a break and I noticed the hum had gotten louder. Nothing registered on our pads as far as vibrations or an origin for the hum. We moved farther into the cavern and in the middle of the largest domed area we saw a large, dark blue globe. It was set on a large stand like a giant snow globe. As Tanner moved in for a closer look, the globe started to glow brighter. She backed away and it dimmed. I moved toward the globe and it started to brighten again. We all realized that it was some kind of test, so Marteen moved toward it and it did not brighten. The same happened with Baskin. Saunders and then Caspian approached the globe with the same glowing effect. I knew for sure in the pit of my stomach that the globe was related to the Eleusians. I approached the globe and touched it. A loud noise flared up and the globe began to turn from a dark blue to an aquamarine color and then a bright green. We backed away as the globe started to vibrate and the its surface texture changed. The top section of the globe stretched in an upward direction as if something was trying to get out. I raised my pad to take radiation readings and saw it was the same radiation as the blood samples from Marteen's people, but much higher. The top of the globe began to change shape. It changed color and protruded upwards as if something was coming out. The protrusion was turning from a blue to a silver color. The object coming out of the top of the globe was forming into a head and shoulders, then the rest of the body rose up and came out like some kind of alien birth. The body floated above the globe and the gently came down onto the ground. The silvery coating the covered the body came off as it landed on the mossy cavern floor. We approached it carefully. I pulled out a portable medi-scanner and scanned the figure. It was alive but in a state of suspended animation. I suspected who this might be but I kept it to myself for the moment. The other came closer. Tanner spoke first. "Doctor, is he alive?"

"Yes but he's in some kind of hyper sleep, suspended animation." Marteen came up and confirmed my suspicion of the person's identity. "It's Marcus! How in the world could he have been here?"

"I don't know but we need to get him back to the Kennedy."

The security detail served as orderlies. Tanner signaled the shuttlecraft and they landed at the bottom of the initial entry shaft. The markers made the rescue operation much faster and about two hours later, Marcus was on the ship, in quarantine. Marteen, Baskin and three other of the elders came aboard as well.

September 23, 2169 1503 Hours

I ran a battalion of tests on Marcus and learned a great deal. First, he had not aged a day since he fell into the cavern. It had been eight years and he had no signs of normal organic decay or even a bowel movement. It was as if he stopped aging on the quantum level. Marteen said he was terminal with colon cancer but, like the rest of the Tempest crew I found no trace of cancer of any kind. It raised more questions but I had a feeling about where we might find some answers. I was going to talk to Tanner but I decided to run a few more tests. Marcus was still in quarantine when he began to stir. I quickly put on a decon suit and went into the chamber. After tossing and turning for a minute, he finally open his eyes. I looked at him and he was scared. He spoke with labored effort and a hoarse voice. "Where am I?"

"You are on the USS Kennedy. My name is Dr. Obama. Try to relax."

"What happened to me?"

"I was hoping you could tell me."

"Captain Marteen, where is Marteen?"

"I will call him. Just rest for a moment." Marcus nodded and seemed to relax. I went to the comm and called Tanner. "Marcus is awake and he's asking for Marteen."

"Acknowledged. We'll be right there."

I looked over to Marcus and he heard. I stayed with him as I reviewed the test results. The most alarming data came from the tests. The benevolent Element X was not only prevalent in Marcus's body, it was off the charts. The radiation levels in his body were almost that of a pure isotope of the element. I was still processing the findings when I noticed a glow from behind me. I spun around and Marcus was floating and glowing. It took me by surprise and I approached him carefully. He looked like he was in a trance and then closed his eyes. He came down slow back onto the bed. I immediately ran another scan and noticed that Element X radiation had gone down considerably. Marcus opened his eyes as Tanner, Marteen and Baskin came into sick bay. Marcus came out of his trance. "What happened?"

"You were emitting some type of energy. You were floating above the bed and glowing."

"Really?" He seemed relieved. Then he looked like he was feeling pain. "I feel strange. My chest hurts."

Marteen, Baskin and Tanner were on the other side of glass. They watched as Marcus writhed in pain. The symptoms were familiar. I administered a pain reliever and Marcus relaxed. His body continued to change into a feminine form. His transformation was the fastest I had seen. For those of us who were victims of the Eleusian Effect, we knew what would come next but fortunately this time, we were prepared. I left Marcus and he was practically female by the time I got out of my protective suit. I spoke to Tanner. "I need to talk to you, quickly."

"Will you excuse us?" Tanner had her diplomatic voice on. "What's happening?"

"Marcus is changing into a female, like us. But it's happening fast."

"What should we do?"

"We have the cure so we can turn him back into a male. So the situation is not as dire as when we were exposed."

"But?" Tanner shifted her stance to her other hip.

"Marteen and Baskin have seen him. They are watching him change as we speak. The question begs, do we tell them the whole story. We need to know what that globe is and how it got here. Marcus was inside of that thing so he's our best resource. It's your call."

"They've spent a long time without a lot of answers. Make them understand how sensitive the information is, but tell them."

I walked back to Marteen and Baskin. They were shaking their heads and trying to make sense of what was happening to Marcus. I approached them carefully. "You have questions. Ask."

"What is happening to him?" Baskin was confused and tearing up.

"We call it the Eleusian Effect. If you will come to my conference room, I will tell you the whole story."

Chapter 20

THE WHOLE STORY

Marteen and Baskin sat for a moment as I accessed the classified drive from the conference room. "What I'm about to tell you is highly classified. We've decided to tell you because both Captain Tanner and I feel you deserve to know the whole truth. The thing is that many lives depend on the keeping the secrecy of what I am about to tell you. This is especially important if and when you decide to return to Earth. Now," I accessed the Eleusian hard drives. "You won't mind if I give you the short version. Three months ago, this vessel traveled to Venus for the first time to do a standard planetary analysis. We experienced an anomaly like nothing we've seen before. We recovered data and technology far beyond own and we've been studying it. Several of us were exposed to a contagious, alien virus.

The virus had caused a catastrophic physiological change to the male members of the Kennedy. Though it was non-fatal, it created a great many," I paused for effect. "-changes."

Baskin spoke first. "What kind of changes?"

I put up Tanner's picture as she is now. "This is our Captain, Deidre Tanner." I brought up another picture of her, pre-Venus and superimposed it over the female Tanner. "When this ship left for Venus, she was a man named Benjamin Tanner."

They were both skeptical and then incredulous. "I don't understand. What happened?" Marteen was trying to make sense of it.

I continued. "When we landed on Venus, the Kennedy had a complement of 235 crewmembers, 15 female, 220 male. We experienced some alien technology and an alien virus. Though I am skipping a lot of information, that virus changed the 220 men into women, fully complete women."

Baskin reacted. "That's incredible! How? I mean how can a virus make a complete chromosomal conversion?"

"We studied the data left by the Eleusians and found a cure. Unfortunately, we found out too late the cure must be administered within the first 30 days to reverse the process or else it becomes permanent."

"So Marcus is changing into a woman but it's reversible."

"We think so, however, he has been inside that globe for a long time so I don't know what effect, if any, that has had on him."

"What should we do?"

"Well we have some time to treat Marcus and change him back, if he wants to."

"What? What do you mean, 'if he wants to?'"

"Well," I paused for a long time. How do I tell Marteen that Marcus is physically enhanced by the Eleusian virus and may like being that way better? "There are unexpected benefits to being altered by the virus. For instance, our stamina, musculature, immune systems are all improved by about 400%."

"You mean he is a better specimen as a woman than as a man?"

"Yes. The Eleusians developed this compound to make better warriors. They were extremely successful. Their women were genetically superior so they geared the compound to the females. The problem was that the Eleusian females were immune to the compound and so they exposed the men. Turning female was actually a side effect."

"So now what?"

"We monitor Marcus for a few days. No longer than a week. Then we start the curing protocol."

"Can we talk to him?" Baskin was anxious.

"Of Course. But remember his situation is very different. Plus he hasn't had any human contact in several years. Only a few minutes with him, okay?"

"Sure, Doctor."

The Elders stayed in the conference room and spoke with Tanner as Marteen, Baskin and I went back to sickbay. Marcus was awake and resting comfortably. I motioned for Marteen to stay back to avoid contamination. Baskin and I entered the chamber without suits and Marcus sat up. I moved in close. "How are you feeling?"

"Better. Amazing in fact. I'm starving though." His voice was significantly higher and feminine.

"No problem, just use the pad and order anything you like. The cantina will send it up to you."

"Thanks."

Baskin moved in closer to the bed. "Marcus, what's the last thing you remember?"

"I remember we were exploring the cavern and there were the big pits. I climbed down to a ledge and realized I might have been in trouble. I saw something glowing in the pit, and an energy told hold of my brain, like a massage and it felt amazing. Before I knew it, I was falling."

"So you were awake when you landed?"

"I think I hit my head on the way down. I don't remember hitting bottom."

"Anything else?"

"I remember the sensation of floating. I figured it was you guys bringing me out."

"All right. Get some rest."

"Wait, I have questions."

"Sure. Shoot."

"Where did you guys come from? Did they send you to rescue us? That doesn't make any sense. What kind of ship is this? How long was I down there?

"Marcus, much has happened since you went missing. Some of it may be hard to accept. Here's what I can tell you: You are rescued and have the option of going back to Earth. The difficult thing is," I paused to let Marcus know some difficult news was coming. "The thing is you have been down in that cave for eight years."

All the color dropped from her face. Marcus was pretty, like a female twin of himself. Her hair was shoulder length but unkempt. "Eight years?"

"Yes. Baskin can come in but until we know more about what happened to you, Marteen and any other male cannot come in, at least not without a protective suit."

"Am I contagious?"

"In a sense, yes but we have some data that may help you understand a little better."

" I don't understand."

"I know. You've been through a trauma that is, to say the least, unprecedented. I will go over the data that we just showed Captain Marteen and Lt. Cdr Baskin. Give me a moment." I left the chamber and got a spare pad. I returned and prepared Marcus for the whole story. "As I told the others, what I'm about to tell you is highly classified and the lives of many people depend on it's been kept a secret." I proceeded to tell her everything that happened to us. I suspect she would take it better than the others and she did. "So you can cure me?"

"Yes. There is time, unless there are complications."

"Like what?"

"We're not exactly sure in your case. You were inside of that alien globe for a long time. We don't know what effect that has had on you. You changed faster than us so we need to study you and do more tests."

"I understand, Doctor."

"Get some rest. We'll continue tomorrow."

September 24, 2169 0512 Hours

I woke up to the sickbay alarm. I threw on a robe and ran down the hallway. The two nighttime med techs were in Marcus's chamber trying to stabilize her. "What's happening?"

"We don't know! She was asleep and then she went into cardiac arrest!"

Marcus's body was shaking violently and then it started to glow again like before. Gradually the shaking subsided but after the lights flashed, our monitoring devices were offline. Marcus began to float in the air but seemed calm. Just then the comms sparked to life and a voice came through. "Bridge to sickbay, bridge to sickbay, come in!" There was a grave sense of urgency in the voice. "This is Captain Tanner, is everything all right down there?"

"We've had a bit of a scare but it's contained. How did you know?"

"A burst of energy came up from the planet. We've pinpointed the origin and its target. It was from the cavern where we found Marcus. "

"Target? Are we under attack?"

"It doesn't seem so. No projectile has been fired and there doesn't seem to be any damage, but the target was the Kennedy, specifically sickbay."

"Okay, let me get back to you."

Marcus was out of danger and our machine came back online. She was floating in a standing position with her eyes closed. She radiated high levels of Element X energy, and landed softly on the floor. When she opened her eyes, they were electric blue and sparkling with energy. She looked around and in a different voice with an unearthly reverberation, she spoke. "I AM THE EMISSARY."

Chapter 21

THE EMISSARY OF TRILLIAN

I spoke to Marcus, now the Emissary. "You are the Emissary?"

Her voice was quieter, but still different from Marcus's. "I am the Emissary of Trillian, originating from Eleusia, but you call it Venus."

"How did you know we called it Venus?"

"This host provides me with all of his knowledge in order to communicate and understand your species."

"Are you Eleusian?"

"Yes. A millenia ago, the Arbiters sent out several scout vessels to colonize and research other worlds. We are a peaceful race but we knew by studying Earth that other species could be violent. Our own race had violent periods so we sought to avoid the mistakes our ancestors made."

"Why are you here?" I felt a strange connection to the Emissary.

"Within each scout vessel, lay an omnisphere, a compendium of our planet's knowledge and culture. It also contained technology that would allow us to connect with the inhabitants of any planet it landed on. We had hoped to build a vast network of communities throughout the galaxy. We would not ever know if we were successful since as the last vessels were launched from Venus, our world was coming to an end. The omnispheres carry the means to integrate elements of our culture, science and technology into carbon based planets and moons."

"Is Marcus all right? Will he live?"

"My time in this host is indeed temporary. He is unharmed as he is aware of everything that I am."

"What do you want?"

"My mission is to enlighten the inhabitants of this world, known to the Eleusians as Trillian."

Baskin spoke up. "We call it Centauri. We live here."

"You are not native to Trillian."

"We are from Earth. Some of us landed here by accident."

"We are aware of your situation. It was the omnisphere that brought you here."

My curiosity was on fire. "Why did you bring them here?"

"They would have perished. The omnisphere detected your primitive vessel and evaluated it. The inhabitants were physically unable to survive the remainder of the journey and Trillian was the closest planet that could support them. The omnisphere imbued the vessel with the sacred energy and brought it to Trillian."

"Did the omnisphere cure us?" Baskin was as curious as I was.

"Yes. Your physical maladies were simple to cure and the atmosphere was adjusted to near perfect conditions for your survival. We only asked for one thing and you provided it."

"What was that?"

"This host body. It was the best way to communicate with you. I am aware you have Eleusian technology on this vessel. I would like to access it, please."

I got the feeling that this alien, the emissary, was becoming more human as time went on. Her demeanor was becoming more familiar and she was sounding less alien. "I will have to check with the Captain."

"Of course. I will await your answer."

"Give me a moment." I walked over to the comm and called Tanner. An orderly showed up with some food Marcus ordered before the Emissary appeared. "Ah finally! I'm starving!" We were all shocked at the familiarity of the comment. It was as if Marcus was back. She took the sandwich and looked at us. "I'm still in here and I'm okay."

"Marcus?" Baskin was relieved but still pensive.

"Yes. The Emissary is sharing me. We are very hungry."

"Weird." I thought.

"This is Tanner."

"Captain, we have an unusual situation in sickbay. You'll want to see this yourself."

"Acknowledged. I'm on my way."

I turned back to Marcus/Emissary. Her eyes were still sparkling but not as bright. She was understandably hungry and was almost done with her sandwich when Tanner arrived. "So what's going on?" The Emissary was facing away from Tanner when she walked in. "I am the Emissary of Trillian, Captain." She turned and Tanner noticed her eyes.

"Okay, what exactly does that mean?" I knew Tanner had to see her as we first saw her. She, sensing the same, she put down the sandwich, lit herself up and rose above the floor. She shone like a star and Tanner understood. Without looking at Tanner, I said, "She is sharing Marcus's body for now."

"Is Marcus okay? I mean is she still in there?"

In a different voice, the Emissary responded, "Yes, Captain and I am fine. This is necessary so the Emissary can talk to us."

I caught Tanner up to speed. "So she wants to look at the Eleusian data?"

"I suspect she wants to see the updates. This omnisphere was launched before the Eleusians died. She may not know that."

"I suppose we owe her that for saving the Tempest. I'll allow it but you'll have to keep close tabs on her."

"Roger that."

Myself, Baskin and Marteen in a protective suit led the Emissary out of sickbay and towards the Science Research Lab. The Emissary studied everything in her path. "You have come a long way since we launched our omnispheres."

Baskin asked nervously, "These spheres are like probes, aren't they?" The Emissary pondered for a moment. "Probes. Yes, I suppose you could call them that."

"Why did the Eleusians send them out?"

"After several millennia of advancing our own technology and culture on Venus, we discovered that we were the most advanced race in the solar system. We sought out similar races and cultures to expand our own knowledge and when there were none in our own solar system, we ventured out beyond it. We knew that not all life forms were like us and they make react negatively to our presence. We created the omnispheres to give us as much information as possible before we made our presence known."

"Did you find hosts on other planets?" I was very curious to see how far out they were able to achieve.

"That is not known at this time. Each omnisphere is sent to a specific system. It evaluates the planets in that system and then seeks out intelligent, carbon based life."

"So you actually don't know if your race found other planets. You only know about this one."

"That is correct. I will know better when I am able to commune with nodes. You have been calling them drives, I believe."

"Yes, they are in here." We arrived at Science Lab and the techs were lining up the drives. We had the chamber sealed for the male's protection since we did not know if the Emissary radiated the same high yield hormones that we did. I wanted to stay in the chamber.

"You cannot." The Emissary was adamant. "It's for your own safety. I will be expelling and channeling large amounts of energy and it is not safe for you. Even in your current condition (as an enhanced female)". I was a little annoyed but complied with her.

We had engineered compatible housings for the drives and there were about twenty of them. Each of the drives were about the size of a watermelon. The material for which they were made was unusual due to its composition and the Eleusian circuitry would not work outside of it. The housings appeared to be as hard as metal but had a waxy, soft plastic feel to them. It was easily reshaped but nearly impossible to change. It would become malleable when heated but it would not melt; it would become stiff when cooled but not break and would return to room temperature almost immediately when the heating or cooling source was removed. The Emissary stood in front of the long table where the drives sat and stretched out her hands. A dark, purple energy appeared and swirled around the room. A cloud of it positioned itself over the drives and extended a ray of energy to each. The energy ran the drives and they vibrated and shook with the intensity increasing gradually. There was a noise, a familiar hum like we had heard in the cave before we found Marcus. The Emissary's body shone like a star as she absorbed the purple energy, which was growing lighter in color. She rose above the floor, floating like a celestial sacrifice. She seemed calm at first, but her face was showing signs of strain, as if she was lifting a heavy load. The light from the energy was growing brighter and it was becoming more difficult to see her inside the lab. The hum was getting louder, too. There was a flash and a loud thunderclap. It knocked out the lights in the lab and everything was dark and quiet.

"Computer! Turn on emergency lighting in Science lab!" I screamed. "Can anyone see her?"

Marteen was temporarily blinded. Baskin was slightly better but still trying to get her bearing. For some reason, I could still see and I tried to open the chamber. The door lock would not budge and the chamber was still dark. I ran to an access port for a laser cutter and cut through the door mechanism. "Computer! Lights on!"

"Unable to comply. Lights are non-functional."

I ran back to the port and got a flood lamp. I shone it into the lab and found the Emissary on the floor unconscious. She was barely breathing. "Obama to sickbay! Medical emergency in Science Lab One. One casualty, send medical team, stat!" I stabilized her as best as I could and attended to Baskin. She was okay and I had her stay with the Emissary. I checked Marteen and other than a slight headache, he was fine. The medical team made it in record time and they brought the Emissary back to sickbay. "I will be right behind you." I hit the comms on the wall. "Obama to Tanner, I need you in sickbay, immediately."

"On my way."

I ran almost full bore to sickbay. By the time I got there, the med techs were already starting an emergency medi-scan. "Her nervous system has been overwhelmed. She'll be out for a while but she should be okay."

"All right, patch it through to my pad so I can monitor it. I'm going back down to the lab."

"Yes, Doctor."

I ran back to the lab and the technicians were surveying the damage. Mostly superficial with the xenon lights blown out. The drives, on the other hand were a different story. Wilson and Jamie Braddock were examining the husks of the drives. "Ruined, all of them." Jamie was more than annoyed. "Fortunately, we were able to back them up."

I was impressed. "So we still have the data?"

"Yes. There's still about 10% of it we haven't gone through. We scaled back analysis when we got to Centauri. The plan was to continue after we had settled things here. I hope that the data will still work. We were pulling it directly from the drives because it was the easiest way to interface with our system."

"All right so things aren't as bad as we thought."

There is an old adage that says not to say things like that due to the perceived existence of a cosmic 'jinx'. Meaning that when you say that things are as bad as they could be, the universe sees that as a challenge to add calamity. Such is the case but not the way you'd think.

Chapter 22

EXODUS

September 27, 2169, 1130 Hours

"She's awake!" The Emissary had been unconscious for three days. I was monitoring her vitals when her eyes flickered open. "I am alive?" Her voice was low and labored.

"Yes. Are you still the Emissary or Marcus?"

"We are both still here. I must return to the omnisphere to transfer the data."

"You need to rest. You've been out cold for three days." I was concerned that my unusual patient may object.

"I do need rest. I will do as you say, Doctor."

That was easier than I thought. I sent the news to the Captain. She responded that we should meet and discuss the Emissary going back to the cavern. I had a feeling that it was important for the Emissary to go back to the sphere, but I didn't know why. Jamie Braddock contacted me and updated me about the Eleusian data. "It seems like we lucked out. The backup drives are working."

"Can you process the rest of the data?"

"Yes. It will take longer, our drives aren't as fast as the originals but we can do it."

"Keep me posted."

I read through some data for about an hour and went up to meet with Tanner.

"Do you feel different since the Emissary came?" It was something that in the back of my mind.

"As a matter of fact I do feel different. Connected somehow. Probably having to do with the Eleusians and what happened to us." Tanner was unusually thoughtful.

"I agree. I have to believe that Marcus, the Emissary are connected to the sphere."

"That means we are too. That could explain that hum we heard. Marteen and Baskin couldn't hear it."

"I thought the same. Do you think it's safe to let the Emissary go back to the sphere?"

"I'm not sure. Braddock is still working on the last of the Eleusian data."

"She called the planet 'Trillian'. I would think there would be other life on the planet besides Marteen's people."

"We have only the initial scans to go on. We should set up expedition teams to explore the rest of the planet. Let's talk to Marteen and the elders to incorporate their knowledge; maybe they'd be willing to add their own people to each team."

"That's a good idea. They seem to have a handle on the planet already."

September 30, 2169 1330 Hours

After preparing for a multi-team expedition, I went to check on the

Emissary. She was sitting up and chatting with the med-techs about Eleusian history. She apparently was up to speed about the downfall of their civilization and seemed sad about it. I came in with my pad.

"I am clearing you from sickbay. You are free to go, although we have a request."

"What is it?" She had a little of that unearthly tone in her voice again.

"We, meaning the Captain and bridge staff, would like to accompany you when you download your data to the sphere."

"The energy I use to propel myself can only affect my body. I cannot carry people."

"We can use a shuttlecraft to fly with you-or even you ride with us until we get to the cavern."

"That is acceptable. But only the 'enhanced females' as you call them may attend. I fear anyone else may be negatively affected."

"In what way?"

"Males cannot absorb the sacred energy. In your words, they do not have the genetic makeup to handle it. They would die. Your normal females would be sick and infirmed for the rest of their lives. Only enhanced females would be unharmed."

"Okay, I will tell my people."

"Also your shuttlecraft would be destroyed."

"That's a problem."

"I cannot change these facts. I would if I could."

"All right. I will make the arrangements." I agreed with the Emissary that it was prudent to limit personnel for the event. We had most of the original bridge crew briefed and ready to make the trip back to the cavern. Marteen and Baskin had gone back to the Community to prepare a group for the expeditions. I hated to tell Marteen that he could not go. It's like kicking someone out of their house to make repairs. I would tell him when I was off duty.

We decided to launch the expedition early the next morning. I advised the teams to use the rest of the day to finish any last minute tasks and get some rest. I knocked off at about 1500. I was reading my subspace message from my parents and Bill when my comm came alive.

"Lieutenant Conway to Dr. Obama."

"Go ahead."

"Ma'am, I have an incoming message marked urgent from the planet. It's Captain Marteen."

"Put it through."

"WHAT THE HELL IS GOING ON, OBAMA?" Marteen was very angry.

"Whoa, calm down, Philip. What's the matter?"

"I was just informed that we can't be there at the sphere when the Emissary initiates the download!"

"That's correct. The Emissary said it would be harmful to anyone who wasn't enhanced. We have no idea what would happen to you. It's a safety measure."

"This planet has been my home for the last 15 years!"

"I know but we are dealing with technology we don't fully understand yet. I am asking you to trust us. Trust me. Let us investigate this and we will share information and let you and the Community know what happened."

Marteen went silent for a moment. "Okay. I suppose we've waited this long. Let me know what happens."

"I will, I promise."

"It's not fair."

"I know. I wish there was another way. I'm sorry."

"All right. Marteen, out."

I was curious as to why Philip was so hell bent on being there when the Emissary downloads. I went to the bridge and sat at my console. I suppose he is connected to the planet much like we enhanced females are connected to the Emissary. I wondered if there was any information about the spheres and the Emissary concept in the drives. I patched into the Eleusian backup drives and looked up the omnisphere and the concept of the Emissary. The Eleusians had millennia of technologic advances which in essence allowed them to explore the universe, albeit somewhat remotely. The spheres were in essence direct emissaries in the fact that they would assimilate the local intelligent life to communicate and affect them. God only knows how it would affect those lifeforms long term. I read more about the Eleusian's space exploration methods. Their technology was so advanced that it seemed nothing could stop them from exploring the cosmos. Finally I found what I was looking for. According to their Space Directorate, the Eleusians were looking for lifeforms that were similar to them. They seem to believe that there were more Eleusians or cousins beyond the solar system and they were looking for them. Downloading the information was supposed to initiate some sort of wormhole and be sent back to Venus. Due to the amount of energy it took, the download would only happen when the Emissary could hold no more data. Once the sphere was activated, an inner pod would receive the data and separate from the sphere. The sphere would then convert itself to some type of mechanism and it would generate and expel a mass of energy in order to send the datapod back to Venus. All of a sudden I felt queasy, like a terrible cataclysm was coming. I spent the next few hours trying to determine how much energy would come from the sphere when it was ready to send the datapod home. Once I processed my findings I was horrified. I called Jamie Braddock to check my findings. "The math checks out, Doc."

"Is it really possible for the sphere to generate that much energy?"

"As you said yourself, we are still learning about the Eleusian technology. It took eons for them to design this thing. There's a lot we still don't understand."

"Most of what I found flies in the face of conventional physics. We have to be positive about this."

"I guess one more person could check it."

"Tracy should. She's as good at this stuff as the rest of us."

"I'll call her."

As I suspected, Tracy confirmed my findings. I felt bad because it meant uprooting the Tempest Community. I called Tanner and had her come to my console. We moved the discussion to the conference room to discuss the next move. "Marteen isn't going to like this." I mused.

"He's not going like being vaporized either." Jamie said with a low voice.

Tanner started to pace. "Is there no other way? I hate to make those people move if they don't have to."

Tracy spoke up first. "Captain, all three of us checked the data. We've run all sorts of computer simulations and checked all the calculations."

"All right. Let's contact the Community. We need to act fast if we're going to save those people."

The Captain dismissed us and we got to work. It took the rest of the night to get sections of the Kennedy ready to receive the Tempest Community. By morning, we asked the Tempest Elder's for a meeting with everyone in the Community and the science staff of the Kennedy. Though bewildered, the Elders agreed to a mass meeting. It would be a historic moment.

Chapter 23

A GRAVE DECISION

October 1, 2169 1000 Hours

I grabbed a couple of hours of sleep and then got ready for the meeting on Centauri. I met up with Tanner, Jamie, Wilson and the bridge staff. I had a few med-techs on hand just in case. We shuttled down to the planet and met with Marteen and the rest of the Community.

"Come to Order." Marteen was unusually formal. "This special meeting is now in session." Everyone sat down. "The Elders have called this meeting because the fate of our Community is at a crossroads. As you know, The Emissary, Marcus, has been changed, altered in a way we still do not fully understand. The omnisphere is a probe from Venus and the Emissary needs to download her information to it. The problem is that once the download is complete, the resulting energy discharge will destroy this planet and everything on it." The crowd murmured with concern. Many were questioning whether or not to let the download happen. Marteen called for order and continued. "We have a choice to make as a community. Now we were considering returning to Earth with the Kennedy; we may not have a choice now."

A man from the crowd spoke up, "What if we don't want to leave? We have a nice working society here. Why does it have to change?" Tanner spoke. "I know it's a difficult matter. It was never our intention to disrupt your lifestyle, however, you may need to leave Centauri whether you want to or not."

A woman spoke up, "What do you mean? Are you going to force us from here?"

"That is not our intention. The problem lies with the Emissary. She has become a being of great power and she needs to expel the data within her else she could become critical."

"Critical? Like a bomb?"

"Yes. Fortunately, we analyzed the data from the Eleusians and this is what we've concluded."

The crowd murmured again. Tanner continued, "Her genetic structure has been greatly altered. I'm not sure she could stop it if she wanted to; the way we understand it she must evolve. The only way she can do that is to connect with the omnisphere and download the data that is written into her DNA."

Another woman spoke up, "So we have to sacrifice our planet and our way of life to this Emissary?"

It was my turn to speak up. " You aren't sacrificing the planet. It's an unfortunate process that has to take place. It's not like anyone knew about this. The Eleusians set up this method of exploration millennia before any of us were born. It may have happened whether we discovered it or not. The upside is that we discovered it in enough time to do something about it."

One of the elders spoke up. He was chief engineer of the Tempest,

Walter Blake. "So, if what you're saying is true, this planet is doomed."

"Yes," I said solemnly. "You'll have to come with us. Once you are safe, we can discuss your futures."

"Is there nothing we can do? Baskin had been quiet for a long time. "The Earth has changed. We really don't belong there anymore."

"I wouldn't say that." Jamie Braddock was unusually optimistic. "You survived on an alien planet with next to nothing and did pretty well. Assimilating back to Earth should be a lot easier. You may even have descendants there. Isn't it better than the alternative?"

Tanner piped up. "There is another option. Those who are interested in joining GASA might be able to stay with us on the Kennedy."

Marteen spoke. "Some of the youth expressed an interest in exploration. That may be another alternative."

The Elders chatted between themselves and then spoke to Marteen. He turned to the community and said, "The Elders will hold a closed meeting to discuss our options. Captain Tanner, how much time do we have?"

Tanner turned to us and confirmed the time left. "You have 48 hours. Please decide quickly. My crew has orders to leave orbit immediately once the download is finished. There's only a small window of time to escape the blast once the Emissary is finished. Once we are clear, we will monitor the discharge from a safe distance in space."

"We understand, Captain Tanner." Marteen was solemn. We went outside and headed towards the shuttlecraft. We took a moment at the shuttlecraft before getting in. "What do you think, Captain?"

"I have no idea. I'm hoping they just come with us, but I'm sad that they are being forced to make the decision. I have to believe that after all they've gone through, the choice would be simple."

"The planet has so much potential. But-" I started to ponder.

"What is it?" Tanner asked.

"Isn't it strange that the Eleusians put all this effort, science, technology and time into space exploration but made no provision for the inhabitants of the planets they explore to survive their download? I mean they must have known what would happen when the planets' emissary would merge with the sphere."

"It's an incredible oversight, if it was one."

"All the data we've have on them, they never came across as

conquerors or destroyers of worlds. I have a hard time believing they were this sloppy."

"True. I guess they weren't perfect after all. It's seems their legacy is flawed."

"I suppose. What about the community? Do you think they'll come with us?"

"If they believe what we're saying; they've survived through a lot adversity. I can't comprehend that they wouldn't."

"I agree. I guess all we can do is wait."

I went into the shuttlecraft and accessed the Eleusian drives on the Kennedy. I had a suspicion about the nature of the whole Emissary process and after about ten minutes of research, it seems my suspicions were correct. I called for Tanner. "Captain? A moment, please?"

"Doctor."

"Take a look at this. The reason that the Emissary process is cataclysmic is that it's the first one."

Tanner realized what I was saying. "You mean this is the first Eleusian download off-world?"

"Yes. The Eleusian civilization was in the process of collapsing when their scientists launched the omnispheres. They were only to launch a fraction of the spheres that they had planned. They were literally attacked and slaughtered as they reached into space."

"Incredible. I'm not sure that that will sway the Community one way or another."

October 2, 2169, 0823 Hours

As we waited for the Community's decision, we readied ourselves for a fast exit when the download was complete. I was in sickbay when Tanner called. "Danna, the Community just contacted me. They have made a decision."

I held my breath, "What did they decide?"

"They're coming with us. They are evacuating the village now and are set to be aboard in 12 hours."

I exhaled. "What a relief. I just couldn't see any other option."

"Me too. Marteen said it didn't make sense that after being completely healed of their illnesses, that they would throw it away by staying on a doomed planet. It was a hard decision, I imagine but I think it was the kids that helped them make it. The elders wanted the children to survive and the children would not leave without the elders."

"It's nice they are so close."

"Danna, just make sure the males are protected from us. They are used to a lot of fresh air and a clean environment. I don't want any spontaneous gender changing happening."

"Will do."

I checked the pheromone blocking protocols and the balancing mixture. Everything was normal but I decided to have all the men from the Community inoculated just to be safe. We knew that they all had been exposed to Element X and the Omnisphere was the source. I programmed the medical server arrays to adjust for Element X and also to red flag any significant hormonal or pheromone fluctuations. I contacted Operations to make sure we had accommodations for the Community and we pulled several tons of organic food material from the planet as well.

The day went by fast and it was down to an hour before the Community was scheduled to be picked up. The download was scheduled to happen early the next morning. Things were progressing but tense.

At 1900 hours, the first shuttle went down to the planet. Marteen had required the Community to travel light; only the most important things were allowed to come aboard. Food, water, clothing and a keepsake. We provided luggage for them and the boarding went smoothly. At 2110, I checked in with Marteen and the Elders.

"How's it going?"

"Fine, we should only have one more shuttle trip." I saw that Marteen was sad.

"I'm sorry you have to leave your home. It must be hard."

"Thanks. It was hard. We had a peaceful, calm life. It's like we retired to Hawaii. But, in a way I'm glad."

"Why?"

"The children. They didn't have any other future than just surviving. We are all explorers at heart. It's why we wanted to go into space. We figured, if nothing else we could see some of the universe before we died of our illnesses. Now, not only do we get a second chance at life, we have another chance to explore, and now the children do, too.

"That's a nice sentiment."

"Thanks. When is the download happening?"

"Once everyone is off the planet, we will bring the Emissary to the cavern and she will connect to the omnisphere. Once she separates herself from Marcus we have a seven minute window to get Marcus and get back to the ship."

"Seven minutes? That's cutting it close."

"It's the best we can do. We've tweaked a shuttlecraft to make the delivery. We pulled all unnecessary equipment off and reconfigured the engines for speed. We won't have time to test it but my engineers are confident it will do the job."

"Thanks, Doctor. I don't want to lose anyone after we've come this far."

I smiled my prettiest smile and went to my quarters. I decided to make a subspace video just in case. "This is in case our current mission fails. The chances are slim but I still feel I need to make this video. We will be witnessing a most unusual event where an alien life form will literally 'download' her genetic information into what has become known as the omnisphere. Technical data will follow but it's like a probe to search out and connect with living, intelligent life on other planets. The download will cause an immense discharge of energy that will destroy the entire planet. We have found out that this is the first time this event has occurred and the technology is Eleusian in origin. The technology still fascinates us and sometimes confounds us. We don't know if there are any other omnispheres out here but at least now we will know what we are dealing with. On a personal note, I am concerned about us not being able to outrun the blast; if so then I will archive this video. If not, and we are destroyed, please tell my family I love them and Bill, I love you very much. This is Doctor Endana Obama, Chief Medical Officer for the USS Kennedy. God Speed."

I thought that the video might have been too dour for the situation but there's an old GASA saying that says, 'Anything can happen in space. Anything.'"

Chapter 24

THE GREAT DOWNLOAD

October 3, 2169 0004 Hours

It was just after midnight and the last of the Community had arrived on the Kennedy. I went to the Emissary's quarters to tell her the news. I rang her bell but there was no answer. Concerned, I activated the security override and opened the door. She was floating over her bed, glowing with energy. She slowly descended onto the bed and the glow dimmed. "Sorry to alarm you, Doctor. I am ready."

It caught me off guard but I quickly regained my composure. "Marcus will be okay, right?" I sounded like a concerned family member.

"Yes, but you must retrieve her immediately. Once the download begins I can neither control it, nor stop it."

"I understand."

We left the room and proceeded directly to the shuttle bay. The delivery shuttle was ready and we had security on hand. "Everything is fine, stand down." I was slightly annoyed about security being there but it was protocol. Tanner was there. "How are you holding up, Doctor?"

"I'm fine. I'll be glad when it's done though."

"Me too."

As we performed last minute checks, I sensed something. Some projectile was hurtling towards the Emissary. All of a sudden an arrow plunged into the Emissary and pierced her shoulder! "Give us back our planet!" A small group from the community had smuggled some homemade bows and arrows aboard the Kennedy. They were perched on the mezzanine above the shuttle bay floor. Marteen had turned to see it was the few that didn't want to leave Centauri. He desperately called out to them, "You must stop! We don't have time to waste!" We all took cover and Tanner called for security. Two Security officers handled the small group and Tanner ordered them to the brig. I attended the Emissary. "You're bleeding, I need to get you to sickbay."

"There is no time. I can stabilize myself."

"But-" I was interrupted by a glow from the Emissary's body. The bleeding subsided but she was still weak. "Get me on the shuttle." The pilot and I helped her onto the shuttle. Tanner spoke, "Once you let her go, you're only going to have about seven minutes to clear. That energy wave is going to move fast! Get Marcus and get out of there, that's an order!"

"Yes Sir!" The pilot responded out of habit in the masculine. It was a small detail and quickly forgotten once we fired up the shuttle's beryllium drives. "I'll need you to co-pilot, Doctor."

"Roger that. I am also arming the laser cannons, just in case."
"Good idea." We skipped the typical launch protocols and left the shuttle bay. Landing protocols we put into place to avoid skipping off the atmosphere. We risked it and headed straight for the cavern entrance. We hovered above the cavern and put the Emissary into a harness. Once we secured the winch and harness, we took the weight and sent her out, down below us. We weren't sure what would happen next and fortunately the Emissary took over. With the harness still attached (in order to retrieve Marcus, once the Emissary separated herself), the Emissary stretched out her arms and legs and began to glide down into the cavern. We doubled the length of the cable and sent a camera drone to follow. Via the drone, we saw the Emissary's view of the cavern, and then we saw the omnisphere. As the Emissary drew closer, the sphere grew in energy and changed color. It went from royal blue to midnight blue, then it grew lighter and lighter until it was a bright, blazing white. Watching it through the drone, it was still hard to see due to the blinding white light. We adjusted the filter and could see the Emissary creep toward it. Finally the sphere began to elongate, as if to match the size and shape of a person. It morphed into a coffin like shape and surrounded the Emissary. The harness dissolved and we saw the Emissary merge with the now coffin shaped mass. "Shuttle One to Kennedy! The harness has been severed! We no longer have a hold on Marcus!"
"Has the Emissary downloaded to the sphere?"
"Yes. She has merged with it."
"Then depart immediately."
"What do we do about Marcus?"
"Nothing. Get out of there."
"This is Doctor Obama. We made a promise to the Community we would bring Marcus back."
"I know Doctor, but if you can retrieve her remotely then I'm not willing to lose you too. Get back to the Kennedy, that's an order."
"TANNER!" I was incensed. "Didi, we have to try and save her."
"Danna, I can't lose you. You have three minutes to get back here."
I was using pure adrenaline now. "Get me a jetpack."
:Doctor, you heard what the Captain said."
"I know what the Captain said, we have three minutes. Get me the jetpack, now."

The pilot handed me a jetpack. It takes three seconds to initialize so I pressed the start button and jumped out of the shuttle. I fell about half a mile before the pack fired and I barrel rolled to orient myself. I used the drone as a homing pigeon and flew right to the sphere. I could barely see but I found a body on the ground below the floating mass. I strapped it to my own body and blasted out of there. I flew up to the shuttle and crashed inside of it. "GO!" I screamed at the pilot and he pulled the shuttle up almost vertical. Marcus and I fell to the back of the shuttle and bounced around. I was able to look out of the window and see the cavern light up with energy. I scrambled to the co pilot's seat and contacted the Kennedy. "Prepare shuttlebay for crash landing! We don't have time to make it pretty!" I checked the aft view and saw the entire planet glow. We aimed for the shuttlebay which was filled with a special high density liquid foam that firms up when subjected to high impact. We clipped the edge of the shuttlebay entrance which threw us into a spin. We sailed into the foam and bounced off of the back wall of the bay. The three of us were banged up but alive.

"Cutting it close aren't we, Doctor?" The person pulling me out of the shuttle was Tanner. "Just keeping my word, Captain."

"The planet has been glowing white for two minutes. That's longer than we calculated."

"I think it was a gift from the Emissary. No one could have known that the harness would be affected that way. She bought us time."

"Did you know she would do that?"

"I had a hunch."

Tanner called the bridge. "Mr. Sullivan, get us out of here."

"Aye, Ma'am."

Marcus was rushed to sickbay. She had not regained consciousness but she was alive. Tanner insisted that myself and the shuttle pilot get checked out. We had a few bumps and bruises but we were unhurt. I switched on a view screen of the planet and it was still glowing white. The energy readings from it were fantastic to say the least. Tanner moved the ship out another million kilometers that we had originally thought was safe. We watched the planet as the white color started to streak with reds, blues and finally dozens of brilliant, bright colors. It was a symphony of light and then a strange thing happened: the planet disappeared from sight. Then a blinding explosion erupted and shook the entire cosmos. I checked the movement of the Kennedy and we had already jumped to lightspeed. I ran up to the bridge. "Doctor, glad you're here. I need to brief the executive staff immediately. We don't have time for formality so I will just say it. We are not out of the woods. The residual energy from the explosion, is, well chasing us."

"Chasing us, Ma'am?" I hadn't seen Wilson since before the download. "How? Why?"

"My guess is that it's attracted to the ship. I plotted a course to another system to see if we can use a star to distract it."

"That makes sense. How long til we get to another system?" I hoped for quick resolution.

"About four hours at FTL-1."

"That's not far enough to another system." My resolution may have been too quick.

Tanner took a deep breath. "I realize that. I am hoping it doesn't wreck this system. There is not enough time to work it out. We are going to have to wing it. Get all the bridge staff up here to work on this."

"Aye."

After two short hours, we had a working plan. We would fly the ship towards the sun and pull away at the last minute, sending the energy mass into the sun. Hopefully the laws of physics were stable but to be honest, I wasn't sure. I was a loose plan but viable, meaning the only plan. We presented it to the Captain. "Okay, sounds good. Helmsman, how long will it take to get to the sun?"

"At full speed we can orbit the sun in 20 minutes."

"Change course for the heart of the sun. We can't afford to have that thing skip off the sun and come after us."

"Aye Ma'am."

"Course laid in, Captain."

"Engage, full speed." Tanner walked back her command chair and sat down. "View screen, normal magnification."

"So now we wait." I was trying to remain calm.

"Yes. It will be the longest 20 min-" Tanner was interrupted by Tracy Felloner. "Captain! The energy mass is gaining speed!"

"What? Is that possible?"

"Apparently. It's picked up speed and headed straight for us!"

"Time to impact?"

"12 minutes!"

"We won't make it to the sun at this speed." Tanner tapped the comms, "Engineering! We need more speed!

Terry Harrison responded. "She's already maxed out all six engines! I don't know if we can-"

"Find the power somewhere! If you don't we are all dead!"

"If I can shut down some non-essential systems, botany, science labs I may be able to divert more power to the engines!"

"DO IT!" We waited five minutes and then we felt a surge of power. The ship vibrated as it limits were surpassed. The hull groaned under the stress of the added power and for a split second I thought of the resulting damage. When we got close to the pull up point Tanner commanded, "All hands! Brace for evasive maneuver!" She mashed the buttons on her console and the emergency command module rose quickly out of the floor in front of the Captain's Chair. She pressed her hand to the security plate and grabbed the joystick. Evasive maneuver in 3-2-1!" She yanked back on the joystick and the change inertia threw all of us back, even though we were strapped in. The view screen was in real-time so we saw the sun drop and disappear. The Captain eased back on the stick and brought the ship around on the other side of the sun. We saw the energy mass splash over the sun and dissipate. "Terry, give me a status on the Energy mass."

"There is some residual energy," she paused. "But the levels are nominal. We did it!"

Tanner slumped back into her chair. "That was close. Is there any change to the sun condition?"

"No Ma'am, the sun is unchanged."

"Monitor the sun's activity and report in an hour."

"Aye, Ma'am."

I unclasped my belt and stood next to the chair. "Congratulations, Captain. Well done."

"Thank you, Doctor."

"I am heading to sickbay to receive any casualties, so far the reports are none. Dinner later?"

"As long as you bring the Champagne."

"Deal."

EPILOGUE

It's been three days since we left Centauri and escaped the mass of energy that resulted from the download. We monitored the sun and there has been no negative effects of our actions. We returned to the coordinates of the planet to find nothing. We realized that the missing planet unbalanced the Centauri System, but nature was slowly correcting it. We deployed a beacon to monitor the changes and warn other ships to not interfere with the system's natural healing process. We detected no signs of Element X radiation and none of the other planets were inhabitable. We decided to continue into deep space but we made sure that the Community had options. Many wanted to return to Earth but they were in no hurry. It was decided that they would stay with us until we came close to Earth. Many of them would need time to mourn the loss of the world they only knew. Others were excited to explore the cosmos with us. Myself, I was a step closer to fulfilling my dream of seeing the universe. I felt, for the first time that I am ready for what's out there.

THE CREW OF THE KENNEDY WILL RETURN IN
"THE NEW EXPLORERS."